I0544190

Storm Trooper

Leon J. Gratton

Grosvenor House
Publishing Limited

The right of Leon J. Gratton to be identified as the author of this
work has been asserted in accordance with Section 78
of the Copyright, Designs and Patents Act 1988

The book cover is copyright to Leon J. Gratton

This book is published by
Grosvenor House Publishing Ltd
Link House
140 The Broadway, Tolworth, Surrey, KT6 7HT.
www.grosvenorhousepublishing.co.uk

This book is a work of fiction. Any resemblance to
people or events, past or present, is purely coincidental.

A CIP record for this book
is available from the British Library

ISBN 978-1-80381-935-8

Chapter One

Tiris Cord Adjusted the strap on his Grav suit and removed his helmet. He then began to remove the rest of his armour and sat at the controls in the small cockpit of a recon ship. It was delta five the one he had made his wings on, He had purposely stolen said ship for its incredible versatile and quick and easy handling. The rest of his squad were in the cargo bay all of them suited in the new K11 armour. It was Terrar's newest armour and the space command had only two units worthy of said armour. And, seeing as Tiris had been Itching to dessert as his squad, had drawn the task to try out the K11 power armour with its reaper shaped helmet.

The skull made the impression of doom for all who glanced at the suit and its macabre helmet. The fact that all the suits were impervious to most weapons that were around in the Empires universe, the K11 armour had got the reputation of being the most sinister and ominous of attire. Apart from the practicality and power of the armour, it was revered as the holy grail of a Storm Troopers life. When you got your first suit of armour, the old K78 power armour, you were blessed, but this armour was the crème da la crème.

Tiris smiled as he laid his hand on the ships navigation unit and began to key in the farthest point in the Spinward Marches. The ship, a Scout ship, had been through the mill, a number of missions out past the universes markers. They had received the highest Award of Merit in accordance with the Marches Faith Wars, when the Trill had first come out of there corner, disabling and destroying at least half the forces of the Imperium. That was when the Linsani, a Planet of plants and organic life, that had protected the Imperium from the brunt of the Trill's devastating laser lightning weapons which imploded most humanoid's vital organs. The Linsani network were fast onto a dampener of sorts that would stop the devastation that the weapons had on humans.

Tiris smiled as the reactor in the front of the, purged itself and sent the small craft hurtling through the Cosmos. Tiris blew out a match on his old Stoogie. The only bad habit he had and he was glad of its company, He smiled and flicked the com link on to the eight Troopers in the cargo hold.

"Tell Bucker to get on the sand thrower and cover our traces".

Bucker got up and walked to the rear of the Scout ship. He rested his hand on the Plasma thrower and said quietly, knowing if he lit up said weapon the Troopers would be in one hell of a fight. He laughed and said, "Come and get it."

He stopped laughing as did the rest of the Unit when Tiris cottoned onto the fact they were at it. But he held all the aces. He had a kill switch that would kill all of them if he flipped it. It was a failsafe that was implanted into the suits and couldn't be overridden.

"You boys don't get comfortable with the fact that we are deserters, as I could fry you in point three of a second. And I would do it with a smile". He laughed and Bucker did as he was told.

He then rested the back of his head as the purge took into second state, Tiris's grav chair rocked back and he whooped and hollered with his southern accent. "Wah Hooo"

Bucker again put his hands on the Plasma Cannon smiled and thought 'One of these days I'll do it and he will have to face the Imperium on his own, especially after frying us'. He carried on through with the sand thrower dampening the Ion field, making it harder to trace the ship. The Scout ship was heading as far away as he could get. He was determined to pick up some credits on the way to sell the ins and outs of a new Linsani product, one that could throw the whole race of the Trill into extinction. It was called a Medusa seed. It killed at a cellular level, breaking the cat like Trills cells down and turning them into a puddle of blood and moist tissue. It was 99 per cent perfect and there was no antidote (so far). Tiris had already lined up the buyer the head of the trill death squad. Cascoe, a shrewd leader who needed nothing to keep his anger stoked and nothing to keep him ready. When he had come across the death and desolation that was left by the Medusa seed he had turned in silence and left the throws of the Trill society and became super athletic. And super fierce. He vowed to get a hold of the Linsani worlds and leave them in devastating shape.

Tiris prepared himself for the final kick of the engine. Then the ship would use its own inertia to come into contact with the closest of the Trill war worlds, The ship carried on moving at G-force. It did this for several hours then began to slow down, The Trill world of the cat is very strange, they look harmless, look like a race of timid, harmless cats but in fact they were quick to temper and had already acquired several trophies in the shape of scout ships and bloody bones that they kept as trophies after they had dined on the Scouts. Tiris knew this of course but still he thought that extinction of the race would be overkill. He was of the belief they both would have lots to share and that peace would be beneficial to their races. It was a war of faith and Tiris had lost his long ago. The inertia had kicked in and Tiris fell into a sound sleep.

Cascoe picked up the ships trajectory as it drew close to the war world that he was in charge of. He had a lot to explain to his superiors. How he delt with this acquisition of the Medusa seed was tricky and, seeing as it was one of his mortal enemies that was bringing the deadly strain of biological weapon, it was twice as troubling. They had been in contact with each other in secret, using old codes and strange new languages that no one had heard of. They were careful not to override the networks with anything that could be sent back to either of the two Captains. They had built up a rapport, almost a brotherly bond between the two of them. They were hard and fast creatures, the Trill who were known for their ferocity and take no prisoner attitude. They weren't a force to be treated lightly. There weapons were devastating and their coldness in playing cat and mouse with the human forces, had a huge impact on the Scout's and various other travellers.

The fact that the Trill were methodical and just as you thought you had escaped them they appeared and destroyed you, this could be days into the fight, sometimes weeks. Then they would appear and leaving you limping, then they would clean their claws and go in for a nasty kill. This would be the way they fought after the initial onslaught, where they had left the human worlds with about half its forces devastated, that was when Linsani had come into fruition then worked on the organic dampener that could reduce the pressure of their weapons, that was when the K11 armour was in its trial phases. It had been suggested in the ranks that said armour was a myth. It was in those times of trial and error the suit was coming into reality, the skull helmet was the final touch on the armour. The suit itself was black with the white skull, giving of a sinister look that scared most enemies. Especially when it was used to clean up the outward marches, the pirates and various enemies had been made examples of by the two squads of 'Reaper' That was what they were called after the onslaught and the cleansing had begun. The Storm Troopers got a reputation of being immortal. You know being able to handle anything. No fear, and that lead to the reputation of them being death incarnate, once the final cleansing in Pirates space they were sent each the two squads to guard the Emperor and his wife and siblings. The Faith Wars carried on another five years.

That was when Tiris Cord had decided to leave with his squad, yes it was mutiny, yes it was desertion, but Tiris was sick and tired. He had neither the patience nor the time to be on ceremony all the time. And the Faith Wars, well they looked like they would never end both sides of them in a state of stalemate. The Emperor and the High King of the Trill wouldn't budge. Their horns were intwined and neither of them would back down. It was a sad fact that both of them had become war junkies. They had get a fix and that fix was in the form of casualties and acquisitions. It was at the last four war councils that Tiris had been withering on mutiny. His faith in the whole Faith Wars was non-plussed. It was time to leave the planet Terrar (Old word for Earth). And he wasn't one for fond remembrances. So he told the squad that there was a better life for them out with the Imperium. And he was surprised to find that they had been contemplating the same thing as him. So they stocked up the Scout ship, *Casandra*, with enough ammo and weapons to hold the whole Imperium to rights. Then they had jumped into space. They had made a clean getaway. And were on the way to the meeting with the Trill Kill team captain Cascoe.

The meeting was about to make them extremely rich but they were going to be hunted and done for treason as well as the mutiny and desertion. But the credits that they would get would make them kings in their own right. The weapons included a heavy plasma cannon, five single shot rocket launchers, armour piercing and heat seeking. Several heavy mini guns. Several laser rifles with twenty shot battery packs. These could be charged after said weapon was used. They also had forty spider mines. A whole crate of napalm grenades, sixty in total. Also several wicked hand held machine pistol. Loaded with dum dum hollow points. That meant they exploded as soon as they hit their target. They also had tech nine armour piercing rifles with about seven magazine with heavy armour piercing bullets, these were standard issue for each Storm Trooper. The weapon had a very versatile use, which was why it was standard issue and it was a lethal gun that in the hands of the Storm Trooper. Made them maximum kill proficient.

Chapter Two

Cascoe was dining, fresh meat and fresh wine. He yawned a small back of the hand yawn. And carried on eating. Two more days and he would be in possession of the Medusa Seed. The might of the war depended on whether he could get an antidote for the biological weapon. He knew that Tiris wouldn't let him down, he had also procured a schematic blueprint for the K11 Reaper armour. This was being looked at by the Trill technicians. But after thirty days and nights of study they still couldn't come up with a weakness in the armour. Cascoe was part relieved at this, as he didn't relish the idea of going up against the squad. He in fact hoped that they could remain friends after the deal was done. He had a lot of respect for Tiris Cord, and hoped he could at least dine with the Captain of reaper team two and maybe afterwards they could share some stories of valour and courage. He really admired Tiris and Tiris admired him back, but alas they were also bitter rivals in the Faith Wars. And the two of them couldn't escape that fact.

He was of the opinion that this deal would seal the fate of the human race. That was providing that they didn't have the ability to mass produce the K11 armour. But the further into the Faith Wars and the more likely that they would be able to produce the armour, that and the Linsani worlds biological damper. That stopped the majority of the Trills devastating weapons, but even this was only at eighty per cent effective, and they knew that the trill had more tricks up its sleeves. The next two days dragged for both Tiris and Cascoe. Then the ship Cassandra came up on the Trills radar. Cascoe smiled and sent a homing beacon out so the ship could dock and land on the space station Fadious.

The station that had launched the main attack, at the beginning of the Faith Wars. It was the Trills major attack point and also its major defence. It was used to coordinate the most lethal of strikes on the Imperium and had done so to lethal effect. Tiris woke up to the nav computer telling him that they were in the Trill space ports and that they were being sent coordinates to doc in the station Fadious. They followed the coordinates and were tucked away nicely into the station's grav field. Tiris began to change and put on his K11 battle armour. He smiled as he sorted the grav field on the armour this gave a feeling of space in said suit. The old K78 had been claustrophobic to wear but this this suit gave of a feeling of freedom. That was one of the joys of the armour. That and pretty much being invulnerable. They docked and let the grav fields heat up and stop the zero gravity.

They opened the air lock door and walked calmly into the space station. Their weapons slung but ready. They each had a tech nine with magazines a total of seven each, each holding a maximum of fifty rounds. Cascoe met Tiris and gripped his gauntleted hand, The cat like captain smiled through his feline features and said, "At last we meet"

Tiris grinned under his skull shaped helmet, he thought as he shook the Captain of the Trill's hand,

'I could finish this war right now'. He then smiled, 'but then where would be the fun'.

The Trill captain smiled and said, "Would you like to dine with me?"

Tiris looked through his blackened eye ports that showed him the best trajectory for a pre-emptive strike. He smiled knowing that they could take this place apart. But that wasn't in the Storm Troopers best interest. "Why not," answered the Reaper Captain. They all headed through the stations docking lock and into the Trill armoury and assembly points. The surprising thing was that they were vacant, only a couple of Trill kicking about. The rest were for some strange reason elsewhere. Tiris followed Cascoe. With his squad of eleven including himself. He knew nothing would happen but still the fact 'Where are all the Trill Soldiers?' He thought then surmised (and this was true of any army), manoeuvres. They were probably out training and getting ready for their next strike. This didn't worry Tiris as they were fast on being rich and spending the rest of their days on a tech eleven world, living like kings.

He smiled into his comm link. "Right men," he said then switched to inner link so only they could hear, "We are going to dinner then were gone with enough credits to make even the Emperor jealous, But stay sharp, there is something amiss about this". They Reapers all checked in, Bucker was first then down the ranks to private.

"Dayton," check "Artemis," Check "Cauldwell," check "Crassent," Check "Piper," Check "Armstrong," Check "Hue," Check "Samster," Check "Pleasence," Check. They then carried on through to the mess hall which was just as empty as the rest of the station.

They sat down and removed their skull like helmets. And sat and had a pleasant meal whilst, Tiris and Cascoe spoke of past military glory and experience and about the battles they had hardened onto themselves. They were evenly matched, each with their own particular brand of leadership and glory, they spoke whilst enjoying their meal. They, as it had turned out, were both sick of the Faith Wars and were only hanging on for them to finish. But there seemed to be little of a sign for peace, with both sides generating a new level of hate for each other.

They tried a couple of times to bring about peace but both the Emperor and the high King of the Trill couldn't adhere to the signing and enforcing of a peace treaty. No they were both too arrogant and couldn't see a decent way out, other than one side winning and other being obliterated. No the Faith Wars were far from over that is why Tiris and Cascoe were so compatible. I mean they were both ready for all kinds of action, both of them seeing the end of the war being futile and nowhere near close at hand, that was part of the reason that Tiris had deserted and was willing to commit high treason. He knew one day he would end up fighting the Imperium and the other squad of Reapers. That's if he survived this meeting with the enemy of his and the human race. He got to the understanding that Cascoe was bored of military life like him. He even put forth the proposition that he came away with Tiris and his unit of Reapers.

Cascoe merely laughed and said, "That is not possible".

Tiris smiled and continued, "It's just a thought." Cascoe patted him on the back then drank some more red wine.

"I like you Tiris," he said and sipped at the blood red wine. "I would love to be a part of the company with you and your squad of Reapers. But I have family throughout the Army of Trill and they rely on me and my abilities to fight and coordinate this army."

Tiris continued with the meal and had a good time with the Trill leader, then after the meal was over Tiris lit up a stogie cigar that was handed to him by Bucker. He puffed away enjoying the smoke in the militant atmosphere. Then Cascoe looked at the Captain of Reaper team two, and said, "Let's dispense with the pleasantries. And talk real face to face. You have the Medusa seed yes?"

Tiris sipped some wine then puffed on his cigar. "Yeah I have it" said the seasoned storm trooper. "But do you have the credits for the Item?" Cascoe smiled and replied, "of course I have it ready and waiting".

Tiris smiled through the smoke of his cigar and looked the feline dead in the eye "That's Eleven Billion creds. "That's two billion for me and a billion each for my squad" Cascoe waved his hand in a matter of fact gesture and the Trill servant went and collected the credits. Tiris spoke into his intercom and asked Bucker to bring the Medusa seed. Bucker made off to get the Biological weapon that was stored in the hold of the Scout ship *Casandra*. He returned several minutes later. With a black onyx coloured vial that housed the deadly strain of weapon. Tiris took the trill Captains hand and shook it. The trill pointed at the grav field and boxes of the gold credits that were floating on an ion field made stable. This was what kept the Gold credits floating and easy to board onto the Cassandra.

Chapter Three

They left the docking facility of the Trill space station and headed further out into the Spinward Marches. They were heading for a Tech eleven planet. There they would get some work as soldiers of fortune and smugglers. Knowing that this was also Piracy and they would add that to their list of crimes. Tiris smiled and undid the latches on his power armour. He put the suit of armour away in the wardrobe that housed the Grav suit and survival suits known as bubble suits. He punched in the coordinates for a Rygon Five, a cluster of planets that contained the majority share of chemical narcotics. One in particular called Paradox. It was instantly addictive and left the user with the delusion that they were immortal. They would procure as much as they could carry then dock with certain space stations and land on certain worlds selling the substance and tripling their Gold credits.

He smiled as they drew away from Trill space, they all sat back and relaxed, the first part was done. They only needed to procure the highly addictive substance called Paradox. Tiris continued to set coordinates to the base of operations for the control and sale of Paradox, Rygon Five, He told Bucker to take off his armour and dress in civilian attire. Bucker smiled there was no need to be formal, this would be a stroll in the park. No need for the high-tech armour. He smiled and undid the clasps on his suits grav field. Then he sat down at the entrance to the cockpit and strapped himself in and the engines purged themselves again, Straight as an arrow, It would take two days to arrive at Rygon Five. They would then buy up as much Paradox crystals as they could get. Then they would sell it and hopefully acquire a larger ship and begin to run a small but constant operation of narcotics. They would live like kings never want for anything, but space authorities seldom missed a trick. And the Imperium Marines were fast on the heels of Tiris and his crew, but they held fast as they arrived at the Trill corner of space. They knew they were out of their league.

One Trill Battle cruiser locked onto the marine deployment ship *Ofetti*, "you have two minutes to turn around leave the Trill Galaxy". The captain of the *Ofetti* smiled through his teeth and said, "We are chasing known pirates that have stolen a number of highly classified items". The Trill battlecruiser started to count down the seconds as they powered up their gigantic laser cannon. The cannon was on the hull of the Trill Cruiser And could cut through steel like a hot knife through butter. It was one of the more devastating weapons that the Imperium had come to fear. The Navy had lost many men in this deadly game of faith. The only faith you had and this was throughout the known universe was yourself, you soon realised your worth as the man next to you was blown to bits or sucked out into the vacuum of space. Of course sometimes a squad of Marines had ended up getting captured, in which case they ended up on a Trill Warlords plate. It was seen as an honour to be served up to a Warlord and his crew. They rejoiced in the fact they were empowering themselves with the flesh of their enemies. This was an ancient custom that humans had found to be vulgar in the least.

They had passed out suicide pills that the troops were to swallow rather than be captured then after ingesting the poison they would turn their standard issue Las pistol on themselves to cut short their suffering and save them a fate worse than death. Anyway the warlord of the Trill Battlecruiser was still counting down the seconds and he was about to fire the Laser Cannon.

Then Quasti, the warlord of the Trill battlecruiser spoke to the captain Sideso, "You are in Trill space and no amount of political or royal treaties will halt us opening fire". Then there was a sharp blast as the cannon charged up the laser field the waaaahp as it let the deadly beam of light that cut straight through hull of the Marine filled carrier ship. The *Ofetti* began to manoeuvre away stopping the most of the damage but it left the battlecruiser with the loss of thirty per cent of its attack and deployment troops. As well as this, two of its primary weapons (Plasma Cannons) were left detached from the ship. The *Ofetti* was using its sand casters to dampen the laser as it was being aimed at the bridge of the ship, Sideso had a few tricks up his sleeves. He pinpointed the docking ports of the Trill battlecruiser and sent over a detachment of nine, each to three of docking stations. The men were all in full K78 battle armour and each marine was fitted with a Linsani organic, weapon damper. This would render the Trills weapons useless.

They docked and overrode the docking doors then entered, blasting the Trill that were stood there readying to open fire. That was the element of surprise on the humans side. That and the tactical advantage of being immune to the Trills standard engagement weapons. The only other thing they had was hand to hand weapons. And the K78 armour stopped most bladed weapons, short of a chainsaw. Anyway the Marines who would appear to be outnumbered by a full battalion of human eating cat creatures, were about to toss their ace. Two of the armoured Marines had in their possession a grenade with the chemical Medusa seed in gaseous form They pulled the pin smiled and one of them managed to laugh as he said this "Have a nice day".

The toxin went right to work. Leaving nothing but a pool of blood and feline skin. They got all the way to the Trill Warlord and Sideso wanted to meet him personally. He walked through the bloody devastation with his Marine commanders helmet under his arm. He walked right up to Quasti, produced his big bore pistol and said. "On your Knees Cat"

The Warlord did as was asked knowing the outcome to this encounter. The feline warlord hissed through his teeth and said, "get on with it".

Sideso pointed his weapon at the top of the feline's skull. Then blew a big crater in his head. His brains and other tissues splattering over the cockpit of the battlecruiser.

"Now we get to scuttle this pain in the neck vessel."

They wired up the drive of the battlecruiser and set it to obliterate. That meant it would leave nothing but vapour and dust. They set the charges and walked off the cruiser. Then five minutes later, Sideso flipped the kill switch and they carried further into the Trill area of the Spinward Marches. Sideso, standing proud and full of encouragement from his Storm Troopers and the statement that it would make when, it neither showed nor could be reached in any way at all. The high king of the Trill will notice a lack of one of their hardest battlecruisers. With one of their most ruthless warlords being finished and dead, Obliterated in fact. The Ofetti moved further into Trill space ways. He had little evidence but enough of a gut instinct to know that the Medusa seed was only limited because of trading of secrets and chemical samples of the Medusa Seed. Tiris had only sealed the fate of the human race, once they had a way to stop the effects of the Medusa Seed. The already crippled Imperium were going to suffer heavy casualties.

Chapter Four

Tiris Cord sat back as they began their descent into Rygon Five. He smiled and thought about the heavily armed cruiser that he planned to buy with the profits of the first run in Paradox. He would make his and his squad of Reapers, Kings of Space. Which they would enforce with all the might of the new armour they were wearing. They were a combat, kill effective machine of reapers, that nobody could stand against. But they had one thing that could destroy them, and that was reaper team one. Tiris blew out again a match on his stogie. And inhaled the smoke. But this was highly unlikely as the Emperor was Paranoid and fear of assassination kept the first Reaper squad by his side. The ship docked in an air cultivated by a Terra air producer by burning oxygen in the atmosphere. Most People on Rygon Five were too addicted to the crystal produce that they put into their bodies by warming and spiking the nervous system, both parasymthatic and symphatic. It left you pretty hungover and the side-affects were numerous, sometimes paralysis and often death. The drug itself was one of the most lethal recreational drugs in the universe. But when it worked it gave you a feeling that you were invulnerable. But this led to a bad come down, sometimes death ensued, but it was seen as the best high in the universe.

Tiris got up from his rocker chair. And headed towards the cargo bay. The rest of the squad stayed in armour as they loaded the Scout ship Cassandra full to the brim with Paradox crystal. They then stayed a day to recharge their armour and take stock and divide the ammo. They planned no trouble as they knew that the suits gave the right impression that they were not to be messed with. They settled down and put two Troopers on the Cargo doors. They changed guards after four hour periods. They did this four times. Then the next morning came and they prepared themselves for dust off. The purge of the engine and the electronic ion transmitter lit up the Battery, then they began to depart the world, which was a swarming mess of zombies who had neither the energy nor the inclination to rob the Scout ship and well, would you with reapers guarding the cargo hold? The ship was full to the brim with weapons and Paradox crystals. The reapers stood guard and stood fast. They were combat effective and sinister to look at. The sheer presence of the reapers sent your guts turning. It didn't matter if you were wasted on Paradox or some other hyper active drug. You just took one look at the pair of them on guard duty and you knew you had better carry on elsewhere.

They dusted off and headed for another rendezvous where they would dock in a chemical laboratory station, they would have the Narcotic cut in half. They would leave half the product at said station, then take the other half to Quantum Nine. A tech eleven world on the rim of the Spinward Marches. There they would offload half of the product that they had and the other two quarters would be sent into Trill colonised worlds.

They would stand by and wait for the Trill to give them the all clear and then they would land and sell a quarter to the humans worst enemies. The last quarter would be taken to yet another space lab on the edge of the Linsani galaxy. There, they would hopefully be home free and on their way to purchasing a battlecruiser and employing some Scouts. They then would go all the way back to the first chemical station and collect the half of the narcotic. They would sell as they went. That was the plan anyway.

Tiris had it all figured out but something was niggling at him, something that would cause him a world of hurt, but it stayed with him. It was like an itch that just got worse the more you scratched it. They got to the Linsani station when the doubt came into play. The *Ofetti*, which had docked and had major repairs done by Mech Bots. They had limped to the nearest Imperial world and were glad to replenish strength as well as more troops. The *Ofetti* had picked up the Ion trail (even though it was disguised in sand) of the *Cassandra*. Tiris Cord got the warning beacon, as the battlecruiser with enough Troopers to swarm all over them, but they knew they would be wanted alive to be made examples of. The Emperor had been stringent on that fact. Tiris would be beheaded but not before he answered for his crimes of high treason, desertion, mutiny and piracy. The battlecruiser fired a laser across the small Scout ship's bow. This signified that it could blast the reapers to smithereens. But Tiris had a trick or two up his sleeve. He went straight and put on his armour, the armour was fully charged and ready. He sat back down at the helm and began to speed up and manoeuvre out of the Laser cannons range, He then full throttled it to the Trill space, having seen the manoeuvres of the ship and knowing that anything could be waiting in the Trills section of space and he was right, three large warlord class ships were there. He smiled and sent the encrypted message to each of the warlords. They all knew who he was and closed the gap as he passed through like a Hindu cow. In essence they shielded and threw up a stiff front for the small Scout ship, who in turn sped away into the deep space of the Trill. Tiris then punched in the coordinates back to Rygon Five, where he would hopefully buy a new Scout ship.

Money wasn't an issue, they had enough, the issue was whether they would make it back to the Linsani worlds to buy an even bigger ship. It would also take some time to acquire the men it needed to run the battlecruiser. He then punched the auto drive into action and let the ship move through the hyper drive, and into full throttle. He slept the majority of the journey. When he woke he was greeted by the orbital beacon showing that they had arrived. And had a clear landing through the atmosphere of Rygon Five. They landed the ship and immediately Tiris began to look through the spaceport for another ship. The rest of the reapers slept some more, knowing that tiredness kills, leads to mistakes. And they didn't need to be sloppy if it came to a stand-up fight. They may even be equally matched by reaper team one. This may happen any day soon. But they knew if that happened it would be some way to die.

Tiris spotted a class nine recon ship, a bit rusty but still in good shape. She had sidewinder space missiles and a forward mounted plasma cannon. And the new recon ten sand thrower with dual capability. It was a nice ship. And its' name was *ESP*. He struck a bargain for the ship throwing in the *Cassandra* for a sweetener. The *ESP* was theirs and Tiris smiled at the dumb fucking luck that he had at obtaining said ship. It was a bargain at a million and a half of credits.

He removed his skull and smiled at his team, "is she a beautiful ship or what?"

The whole squad applauded silently and to themselves at the sheer fact that a tech nine combat effective Scout ship had just been purchased. And that it was fully armed. They would in no doubt need said ship, as things were getting hairy. They put the last of the Paradox into the holding bay, while bucker inspected the plasma cannon and the state of the art sand throwers, he then looked at the sidewinder space missiles. He had used said weapons a number of times and knew how much a game changer they were. The *ESP* Craft was quite a bargain and Bucker could use the ships armament to full use. Especially the plasma cannons and space missiles. Its apparent state was not too shoddy. It was a little bit old but was still in very good shape.

They strapped in and blasted off the planet that was inhabited by Paradox addicts. It was a good deal and they would have been stuck if it weren't for the quarter of Paradox that they still had. Bucker sat down next to the rear Plasma cannon and sand throwers. Watching their tail as they began their journey to Linsani space. Tiris again stowed his armour in the bubble suit closet. He smiled as the ten reapers fell into a sleep, a much-deserved sleep. Tiris smiled as he struck another match for his stogie. He puffed away for a while then grinned and stretched back in his zero-gravity chair. He then thought to himself about drifting into a sleep. He set the nav computer and main frame for the ships engine to go into automatic and only wake them if in danger of any kind. Tiris settled down and smoked a little more then drifted into a sleep. Whilst the coordinates where passed through the ships main frame computer. "*ESP* Fully automatic" said the electronic AI. The engines slowly heated and cleaned themselves causing the ion field to run at maximum potential. Then the Scout ship headed towards the outer rim of Linsani planets. Then they would sell the last of the Paradox crystals. That would double the profits of the Medusa seed sell.

They then needed to find a home port with soldier of fortune troops and a place to purchase a cruiser class ship and enough people to navigate and keep the running of the ship. Tiris intended on docking the *ESP* on the cruiser and using it as an attack ship if needed. He had been in love with the ship the moment he looked at it. The journey took a day or so and they had no encounters on the way to the Linsani rim. Bucker had stayed awake most of the Journey as he wasn't too reliant on the AI. No, he was always of the opinion that humans were too reliant on computers and Tech. So the survival instincts that he had trained into himself were wholly self-sufficient. And had been honed through countless battles. Not just with the Trill but bug hunts and cyborg renegade pirates. Also he had been decorated with honours, in bravery and duty above and beyond. He was quite the marksman as-well and had saved many a units lives by taking out Trill warlords.

Tiris had never met a soldier more willing to take the fight to the enemy. And they had bonded immediately. Tiris was impressed by the medals a lowly sergeant had gathered. He knew that the man was exceptional in all aspects of combat and tactics. Tiris had spent enough time knowing that the survival rate grew shorter for most troopers. And the Faith Wars, as they were called, were because you had to keep faith in the Universe being your friend and that was all you had faith. But someone like Bucker lived for battle, as did the rest of the reaper squad. Tiris woke just as the proximity alert began to sound. The AI voice was repeating, "Proximity close, proximity close".

The ship was slowing down to let the Reapers get close. "Prepare for manual control," said the AI. Tiris switched on the power up link and asked, "Any sign of hostiles?"

The AI scanned the local area and reported back, "Negative, no hostiles in the quadrant. Just cargo ships travelling to the outer rim of the Spinward Marches".

Tiris smiled and said to himself, "Home sweet home". He then began to put on his power armour. The rest of the squad were beginning to rise from their slumber. Bucker, who had fallen asleep at the Sand Throwers, woke with a small bitter grin. He had all intentions to be ready for the next forty-eight hours, as he was in the state of high alert. And when Bucker was in that state you could be sure he had sensed that trouble was close. And his senses that were keen and battle hardened were seldom wrong. This had been the product of battle and constant vigilance. He was a Trooper through and through.

Tiris looked at the Linsani home world and the huge space station that surrounded the main world. He punched in the coordinates to the space station knowing full and well they would have to be quick in the sale of the drug Paradox. And nothing was surer that after the deal was done they would be lit up like a fresh new day sun. They did what they had to do then left with an obscene amount of credits, more than triple the amount that they had started with. No, if it wasn't at least three times the amount that they had procured from the Trill, it wasn't worth the risk. As in risk versus reward, they were in a short time frame so they docked and sold the cargo then made a healthy departure. Now to the nearest war world, where they would pick up a full crew and a Tech Ten war cruiser.

They arrived at the war world Sigmus Prime, a very advanced world at least Tech twenty-four. They landed on the ground and departed through the cargo bay into the magnificent machine run world, where they would get their hands on the best war cruiser that was known to man. It was official, they were now pirates of the Marches. They would then open up trade as official mercenaries. Selling their skills as a lethal attack squad. And on the side line they would sell Paradox. Tiris began to hunt down a war world trader, the squad looked ominous as it walked in to Sigmus Primes gigantic city, where you could procure anything made of metal or computer synthetics.

There he spotted it, the perfect war cruiser, its name *Defiant*. It had all the trimmings, tactical nukes and high-power Plasma cannons, This war machine could fry half a planet, go away whilst it burned to pick up more Nukes and recharge its Laser cannons and come back and finish the Job. The *Defiant* was a tech eleven war machine. And had several docking ports and twelve survival skiffs, that were able to last three years in deep space. Now he had to find a good crew to man the weapons and keep the ion fields charged. And keep the rest of the crew fed and watered. They had twelve battle hardened technicians who formed squads of fifteen per technician which gave him a full crew of about one hundred and eighty.

Tiris got on board and told Bucker to chase the atmosphere and attach the *ESP* to the rear port when it was getting ready for flight to the Rygon planet, there it would skim the planet's atmosphere and try and find mercenary work. They would stay there until they had enough missions to keep them busy, also small trading in the Paradox crystals.

Chapter Five

The Emperor rose from his silk attired grav bed. He smiled at the three concubines who he had shared the past five nights making love and having sex with. This happened on a regular basis every two or so nights. He had delivered to him three young, beautiful women, whom he had tend to his every whim. They seldom lasted the two days as the Emperor liked it rough, sometimes killing one or two of them. The other was sent away to a drug addicts world, where she would live out a short but pain free life until someone killed her. This was usually over a package of Paradox. And was totally covered up. Even if the news had got out, the networks were run by incapable fat drug addicted spokesmen, who would never bring out the truth about their homicidal, lecherous, sociopath of an Emperor.

They had an idea that they were onto a good thing and played the dumb aristocrat whenever the question was raised. About the missing women they showed expertly detailed camera trickery. Of said concubines, living it up in a utopia of marvellous splendour. They were seen in the Greco-Roman way of life, tending to children having holy days and living a contented existence. But it was all a façade. They were in fact nothing but rotten meat for the Paradox hungry drug addicts. The zombie like state was soon a pale resemblance compared to how the drug changed them. They became lethal killing absorbing bullets and laser damage that did not hold them back. Singular of purpose, feed, spike the nerve, then keep on going getting higher and higher until they fried the central nervous system. Leaving nothing but a shell of a body. Empty void and destroyed.

The *Defiant* lay in wait in Rygon Fives orbit. They picked up a small destroyer limping close to the System of Rygon Five. It was hailing the *Defiant* sending out the SOS beacon to all ships in that quadrant. The ship called the Sidisis was in dire need of help. They had been raided by Paradox meat pirates and they had escaped barely. They were called Meat Pirates because they had more implants and metal bone junk than even the most hardened of Troopers. And were renowned for their bloody capacity for violence and cannibalism. The fresher the meat the more the sweet, that had been scrawled in blood in the cockpit of a Scout ship that had come under attack by the Meat Pirates. The *Defiant* opened up comm links and Tiris spoke to the ship's crew.

"Are you alone, what are you carrying?"

The ship hailed then sent a message back to the *Defiant*, "we are merchant navy and we are carrying surplus food and medicine to the hospital sub-station just four days from here. There were three of us now just us".

Tiris sneered, "Fucking Merchant Navy never short of stupidity".

Bucker smiled and sent the coordinates for one of the docking locks. The Sidisis made the journey and docked in under an hour. The Captain of the Sidisis walked through the tunnel and set the docking clock to pressurise and open in five minutes. The Captain his name Calumn Grievence, was covered in cuts and wounds to his legs that the med bots had seen to. The rest of the crew, the ones that made it were in the mess deck. There was at least twenty who had survived and the rest had been torn to pieces and devoured as the Meat Pirates devoured as they went showing their enemy no mercy and a blatant show of fierce punishment, this had led to most of the security deck losing morale. After witnessing the murderous intent of the cyborg Meat Pirates. They had no chance.

The other two cargo ships had been taken in the ferocity of the scavenger ships. They outnumbered the Merchant Navy vessels three to one. Calumn Shook hands with the reaper teams leader Tiris, then shook hands with the gunnery sergeant Bucker. Tiris took the Capitan to the main deck of the *Defiant*. He smiled and said, "You'll be alright here, I'll send Bucker with the rest of my squad to gather the survivors, we'll patch you up then take you to the med station Gwen".

Calumn nodded his head and replied, "I'll sure appreciate it if you could tow us there".

Tiris smiled and thought, 'What the hell, my good deed of the day'. Tiris handed Calumn a protein blueberry bar and a flask full of water. Calumn sat down and devoured the bar and sank most of the water. Tiris opened up the comm link to Bucker and the rest of the crew. "Take some provisions with you, and be careful".

The nine of them headed with an internal map into the cruiser, it was wall to wall blood and body parts that had been gnawed upon. There were guts and the sour smell of decay, and the blood had already began to separate into plasma, an orange like liquid hung over the doors and covered the floor. But this didn't bother the reapers, as they carried onto the Mess-hall where the rest of the ship's crew had gathered and fought of the meat pirates. They had managed to kill a few, with laser and tech nine pistols. Mostly small arms but they had few small detonators hooked to Plasma Thermite charges. Powerful enough to blow the Pirates to pieces. This was how they maintained a last stand with the ferocious mad flesh eaters. They had set charges and managed to hold their position until they lost morale and gave up. Then they had relaxed in the mess deck. And calmed down. The majority of the survivors were teenage boys and girls, with a few adults milling around, tending to the wounded. They shrieked as the Reapers opened the mess decks doors. Bucker raised his gauntlet and said over the intercom. "It's okay".

He then smiled and started pass out the provisions. Dayton, who was the medical officer, smiled and began to help with the wounded. He removed his skull and started to help with the stitches and staples. Patching up and removing bullets from them. He did the best he could. They had plenty of medical supplies but were low on food. The reapers knew this was just a small amount of wounded and dead they would have to sweep and clear the other decks. This would take some time. The *Defiant* began to tow the Sidisis, toward the Gwen Medical station. It was twenty-four hours away and the coordinates were punched into the navigation console. They then began to move. The *ESP* on the top of the *Defiant*, and the Sidisis on the bottom.

Pig wheeling it was called. It was an old military tactic, that helped strengthen the battlecruisers resolve. Especially in great numbers in the thick of war. These tactics were highly regarded and used mostly in the Faith Wars.

The reapers began their sweep and clear as soon as Dayton had done all he could. Dayton was head of the five-man team Reaper Alpha. And the other five were reaper team Beta. They divided and swept the lower and upper decks each coming into contact with alive Meat Pirates and disposed of them. The small arms fire from the meat pirates had only made the reaper team laugh, but still the meat pirates tried only to be obliterated by the Reapers. This went on for seven hours whilst the reaper team finished off the Meat Pirates. They never knew what hit them. There were a total of twenty of the pirates on each upper and lower deck, the central deck was littered with high explosive shrapnel bombs. This was not even noticed as the armour of the Reapers was impenetrable, and they laughed at the explosion's and carried on until they found the Meat Pirates demolishing squad. There were seven of them holding all sorts of explosive devices, they threw a napalm grenade and Bucker caught it and started to laugh as the thing lit up in his hand. He smiled as the flames deadened themselves and he walked right over the Pirates bodies and got who must have been the leader, as he had more metal parts than the rest of them. Bucker began to squeeze the half metal head with a laser eye and sharp spikes that were sporadically positioned on his head. It began to crunch and tear as the flesh side and metal side were flattened by the armoured hands of Bucker. The rest of the Meat Pirates surrendered to the Reapers.

This gesture of good will was not even on the table and they killed each and every one of them, brutally killed by hand and combat knife. They should have come better prepared though Bucker as he ripped the serrated edge of his knife along the Pirates throat. The Meat Pirate died a little while later, gargling on his own blood. Bucker and the rest of the Reapers enjoyed this, they sometimes wondered if in fact they were immortal.

Obviously, the power armour had gone to their brains and encounter after encounter had only made the Reaper team feel more and more immortal. It was a better feeling than being a success. If only the Emperor had been able to see and feel how good the armour was. He would kit the full Storm Trooper battalion with the K11 armour. But the armour was getting a reputation for being unstoppable. And that is why he kept a Reaper unit at his right hand.

They began to settle on course to the Gwen Med station. Another couple of hours and they would dock and the Sidissi would offload there cargo and be tended by the med stations personnel. They then were surprisingly offered a reward for the help.

Tiris smiled and took the fifteen thousand credits saying, "You never met us, we were never here".

The Head doctor said, "Of course the Sidissi limped here".

"Thanks doc," came the curt reply from Tiris.

They then came out of docking and headed back to Rygon Five. The *Defiant* not a scratch for their first mission. They then got back to Rygon Five and held in space orbit. They then sent the *ESP* for supplies and ammo. They came back a day later. With ammo food and some more sand for the throwers at the back of the

ESP. They settled down on the *Defiant* and removed the K11 power armour and rested. The power armour needed to be recharged every seventy-two hours or so. The battlecruiser, the *Defiant*, remained on alert as Tiris did not trust the fact that they had saved a cargo freight from Meat Pirates. He fell into a shortened sleep with his power armour humming at the rear end of the cockpit. He woke five hours later and there had been no activity, he lit his stogie and drank some coffee. The two things complementing each other, he was happy with the way that his encounter with the Meat Pirates had worked out. He hated Meat Pirates, they were the pain that you couldn't explain. They were all of them hooked on Paradox, that which had turned them insane. Cannibalistic. With a need to enhance their bodies with machine parts.

Tiris wondered whether the other ships that were making the journey to the med station Gwen were destroyed or if they were salvageable. He growled to himself and said, "I hate being a Samaritan", then punched in the coordinates of where they had been sent the distress signal.

"Okay lads that's power enough, put your armour back on."

The squad didn't hesitate, they began to put their suits on and load their weapons. Tiris began to scan the quadrant for other ship activity. He knew that the ships would be left behind as giant tombs with the crew being cannibalized. And the ships left as a warning to everyone else, Tiris spotted one of the cargo ships out at the edge of the quadrant. He punched in the docking procedure. While the *ESP* circled the tomb, scanning it seeing where the Pirates had entered and where they had exited. They boarded the vacant blood drenched vessel. It was dark in the ship and they used their shoulder torches to light up their way. They knew that no one was alive, and that the bodies had been taken for food. They also stripped the shit out of the vessel taking useful machine parts that they would surgically enhance onto themselves. Giving their bodies enhanced strength, hidden weapons like wicked sharp knives and Laser repeaters (Small single shot pistols attached to their arms).

Tiris and his team of reapers made a full sweep of the vessel, found nothing but blood and wrecked ship parts. He noticed that every so often he came upon Paradox inhibiters. This was not unusual for the Meat Pirates. In fact it was like a signature for them. Tiris went up to the bridge and did an internal damage inspection.

"Yep stripped the shit out of it," he said as the computers AI ran through the long list of missing parts. He then tried to locate the cargo if any of it was still around, he doubted it yet "You never know" he said into his com link. Then he asked for the security tapes on what had happened. The AI responded showing security tapes 440, He then watched as the Meat Pirates tore through the very unskilled poorly armed crewmen. They never had a chance. Some of them being gnawed upon as they lay, others captured to be food later on. Some of them stopped to spike themselves with the Paradox Inhibitors. But on the majority it was a slaughter. A mass drug fuelled, cannibalistic surge of darkness. And they left no one in or around the ship. He sat and watched the slaughter then made a copy of the security tapes onto an AI chip. He would show his brothers in arms the whole thing, looking for traits and personalities of the Meat Pirates. How they moved. How they spoke, if you could call the way that they communicated a language, it was usually grunts and striking at their subordinates. The hierarchy was simple and followed simple guidelines, do as you were told and you didn't get eaten.

Tiris soon picked out the leaders. They had the best weapons and controlled the Paradox. If you weren't combat effective you got eaten and your cyborg implants got taken out of you. This happened frequently, and a lot of the Pirates sabotaged other Pirates, giving them the chance at better cyber parts and sometimes they got extra Paradox, only when they were truly treacherous. Tiris watched the whole battle as it had taken place. He noticed three leaders, who were evil and evil through and through. They killed six of their own as a show of strength not only to their own but to the victims of the bloody battle. Who saw the act of aggression and it filled their hearts with fear and dread. The massacre that had ensued on the cargo vessel had put things in perspective to the Colonel. Tiris knew he was going to end up battling with the Meat Pirates. He wasn't scared he had held his own many a time without the armour, under aggressive circumstances similar (If not worse). So he had one choice, and that was to hunt down the Meat Pirates and finish them. And he would do so on his terms of battle. He gathered up the AI chip and headed back to the *Defiant*.

The *ESP* went back to piggy back the *Defiant*. And they left the cargo ship to float in this zero gravity Hell. The Faith Wars would wait. They were too busy to finish off the Meat Pirates, The *ESP* took flight the moment they had a fix on the Meat Pirates position. There were several small ships and one massive, twice the size of the Defiant battlecruiser. It had a bloody streak down it which was congealed blood and leftovers from the twenty or so years it had been travelling. And destroying smaller ships and feeding on the meat of countless victims. Tiris saw the ship and started to laugh. The pirates were about to get taught a lesson. A lesson about who was top of the destroying game, who could set their mark and really enforce it, no he was laughing and so were the rest of the reapers. They knew that this would be a tough but fair fight. Bucker strapped himself into the *ESP* gravity seat. And locked and set the small crafts armaments he was a gifted pilot and knew how to handle a ship-to-ship battle. He had one other person who manned the Sand thrower and rear Plasma gun.

Bucker smiled and said to the rest of the Reapers, "Watch I'll dust three of those little ships and knock out all the ones that come to their rescue."

He set two nuclear sidewinder and a big flash as the Plasma cannon hit its mark and destroyed one of the Meat Pirates scavenger ships. The sidewinders hit the other two and sent off an EMP charge that knocked out all the surrounding small craft. They were dead as doornails and were out the fight. It was five ships dead in space they wouldn't last long either as in their artificial atmosphere you know oxygen would all be shut down. They would suffocate. Bucker knew that that was only one of the tricks up his sleeve. The rest of the reapers smiled and eyes widened at the sheer simplicity of such an attack.

The *Defiant* started to sidle alongside the giant battlecruiser. Close enough to be taken as one of the Meat Pirates scavenged ships. They docked and opened the bridge to the Pirates main vessel. Dayton took point, and the other eight Reapers followed all armed to the teeth with Plasma rifles and small carbines loaded with splitter ammo, a new type of bullet that entered the body then exploded ripping the innards of whomever it struck. But Dayton he had another idea and produced the remote control for the spider mines. He sent them off. Twelve of them went forth, then twelve went to the left-hand corridor and twelve went to the right hand corridor. The Meat Pirates were all playing possum. And hiding in their rooms where they slept and ate. Making out as if someone had beaten the reapers to it. But Tiris had seen this trick played before and it had failed.

The first lot of spider mines went into the living quarters of six cyborg flesh eating Pirates. They stopped in the middle of the room, the pirates thought it was their lucky day. More parts to implant. Then there was an almighty boom and most of the flesh seared and turned into liquid then cauterised and cooked onto the walls. The reapers then began to mow down the survivors. All the while they laughed and fired their splitter ammo. Ripping the cyborgs apart sending organs and metal everywhere. Still the reapers laughed and laughed, they held no one in fear. The left spider mines came into contact with the Meat Pirates in a galley a food hall where they were dining on fresh flesh. The spider mines were barely noticed up into the point when they were detonated. There must have been about thirty Meat Heads and they were busy applauding themselves and feasting on flesh. They were fried and splattered all over the mess deck. The innards hung on to the doorway like dripping confetti and streamers of guts. The ones close to the centre of the room, the ones that took most of the damage were fried and blown to pieces. The smell of cooking flesh wafted right down to the other sleeping quarters, where the Meat Heads were finishing loading their weapons and getting ready by spiking their nervous system with high amounts of Paradox. This gave off the illusion to the Pirates that they were invulnerable.

But the Reapers had other plans. The last of the Spider mines made it to the engine room. They were beginning to heat up when a Meat Head had a thought that he wished he never had to shoot one of the mines, that was a catastrophic mistake. It sent the mines into self-detonate and they all followed suit, wrecked the engine that was old and rusty and in dire need of a clean. It blew huge chunks of shrapnel into the engineers that were doing a poor job but that shut down the atmosphere and gravity. Leaving the huge craft dead in the water the reapers laughed again. They were each of them kitted with state-of-the art Grav boots. That were made for exactly this kind of combat. The Plasma rifles went first. And Dayton came back to the rear. Being that all the demolition work was done for now. They began to pick off Meat Pirates as they tried to swarm the Reapers who made a circle in one of the rooms where the whole ship had access. The Meat Heads were done, they were beginning see the end of themselves as the oxygen ran out. Some of them put guns to their heads, some let off a primordial scream and charged at the Reapers hoping to kill one of the crack elite stormtroopers, The rest tried to jettison themselves of the ship in skiffs. Only to be picked off by the *ESP*.

Tiris fired of his last laser round and started to use his Ripper loaded carbine. The gun rattled and expended the empty casing whist the ripper bullets did just what they were supposed to do, rip the insides of the enemy with a small but powerful explosive charge. That blew the torso to pieces, sometimes two or three times. They again didn't stand a chance as the armour ricocheted their out of date weapons and lasers. Whilst they all laughed as the bodies mounted up and began to float in the zero gravity. That took twenty or so minutes to come to a halt. The reapers welcomed that fact as it made the fish in a barrel saying true. They were gasping for air and had no way to stabilize themselves. It was fun to the reapers. They were in their element, The Storm Troopers finished the whole ship. The *ESP* and the *Defiant* made short work of the rest of the Meat Heads. And their cruisers and monstrous atrocities. *ESP* made light work of the Pirates whilst the rest of them lost morale and headed into deep space. Praying and hoping that the Reapers wouldn't follow. Bucker finished the ones that tried to escape from the gigantic blood-soaked vessel. They weren't too smart. Bucker and the *ESP* went straight to work using as many Nuclear warheaded sidewinders as the ship had, that and the plasma cannon on the front of the *ESP*. The charge ripping through the small skiffs and leaving nothing but charred remains. Whilst the reaper team wiped out the rest of the Meat Pirates. They then headed back to the docking bay and went back to the *Defiant*.

They were still laughing as they left the cruiser, they tossed in Three or four Nuclear detonators. Then they left the dock and blew a huge hole in the under hull. Tiris smiled as the rest of the crew laughed and joked on how they had never seen the likes of the Reapers, And the chief engineer was smiling when he saw the Unit come back aboard. They then went and strapped themselves in whilst the rest of the ship gathered and put the Rygon Fives coordinates back into the AI. The *ESP* Docked again on the *Defiant*. Bucker smiled as the Scout ship powered down.

"Colonel, We need to re-arm the *ESP*".

Tiris spoke back, "First chance we get Sergeant."

Bucker smiled and Tiris carried on. "And sergeant you did good".

Bucker put the switch off on his comm link and headed for the sleep quarters. He met up with the rest of the Reapers. On the way to his sleeping quarters.

They all laughed, "Fucking Cake walk that," said Dayton as he saw the Sergeant.

The sergeant smiled at the Corporal and replied, "Did you think they knew what hit them?" Dayton laughed a short, small snort, and replied.

"No sir no they didn't".

Tiris headed for the bridge. He smiled knowing that they had to make a run to Sigmus Prime where they would reload and refuel. The *ESP* had done its part in the fight with the Meat head Pirates. But had expended most of the Tactical missiles. The run was much needed and it would give the Troopers a much-needed rest, maybe even some drinking time for the Squad of Reapers.

Chapter Six

Meanwhile the Emperor was having a discussion with the leader of Reaper team one. And Alex Cardis. He was a giant of a man, with more battle scars than most. He had several facial scars and a whole heap of body scars, this made him look cold and mean. It was frightening how course and ragged the man was. He spoke with a ragged and harsh accent. Almost like a roar of a lion. He spoke you listened. It was damage that had been done to him when he was just a Private. Chemical weapons and gasses had really made him more scar than human. He liked his scars and so did most of the women that warmed his bed. Some thought him to be ugly and aggressive, others sweet and serene. That trait only came out occasionally and he was fond of being rough and combat efficient in a split second. Nobody messed with him. Alex spoke to the Emperor and gave his much valued opinion.

"If I were Tiris, I would be travelling in a large war cruiser. I know he sold the secrets of the Medusa Seed. He would have made some profit, even smuggle some narcotics to certain worlds where he could live comfortably".

The Emperor smiled and responded in a gentle voice, that was almost a whisper, "He has really shook the tree and watched the fruit fall, then we must act fast".

Alex, Captain Cardis was spot on about the renegade Captain Tiris Cord. He knew several systems where the captain of the reaper team two could hide. The main one was just a small journey just outside Trill territory. The Regis System. Right with the Paradox main world Rygon Five.

"Alex," said the Emperor, who was skinny and lithe and constantly on Paradox. "The Reaper team two must not, and I mean must not, get a foothold in the hearts and minds of my Troopers".

Alex looked directly into the Emperor's eyes and replied, "Yes your exulted one".

He then turned around and headed to his squads location. They weren't happy at the thought of the task. But there weren't any other Troopers up for the task. And knowing how hard it is to penetrate the power armour. They were stuck with the mission. They knew they were only ones capable of stopping the Reaper team two. And the betrayal of Reaper team two had only shown great courage on the traitors part. Nobody had the guts to betray the Imperium and that was a fact.

Tiris knew that it would only be another couple of weeks before Reaper Team One caught up with them. They were in Rygon Ones orbit after a haul over at Sigmus, they re-armed the tactical missiles and gathered up ammunition and laser packs. They also managed to re stock their Spider mines, Dayton was pleased with that. The plasma rifles were set on charge in the *Defiant* and of course they replenished their grenades.

They settled down to a nice cold beer and some local Burgers and chips, It was nice to not be on the clock for the Emperor. They were enjoying their new found freedom and rolling in gold credits. They stayed at Sigmus for a good week or so. Living it up with women, wine and song. Tiris made sure they were relaxed and destressed. They had a large fortune in credits, and they were none so far injured.

Dayton sat next to the Colonel and said, "I take it you are weary of this war?"

Tiris looked at the Corporal, "The moment I put my first suit of Power Armour on I was sick of this war".

Dayton relaxed and they spoke for a good couple of hours, each of them talking about the ravages of war. And how sick and tired they were of taking orders and the Imperium not giving a damn who they lost. Family, friends and loved ones. It was all kept in good Faith. That was why it was called the Faith Wars. You had everything to lose and only had your Faith to keep you alive. Yes the true warrior spirit, you know the man, the soldier next to you. You had each-others backs and sometimes when you were lonely and in the middle of a tour, you had only your brothers in arms. Faith, a funny thing huh. They don't know who started the Faith Wars but it was seen to be lasting over three decades and neither side was going into submission. It was held equal for the two sides. Both holding each other in a military lock. Both having the power yet not the energy to end the war.

They stayed in their Systems with the Trill's being slightly better off. But the Imperium showed no fear. The Generals and Majors, being motivated when they first used the Medusa seed. It was a game changer and showed the Trill that they were outmatched by the Emperor and his Storm troopers. He may not have had the most amount of troops but he had two aces up his sleeve, The reapers and the Medusa seed. But both were about to come into the light and have weaknesses shown. The reapers in particular. The Trill were working on a new explosive that if they hit the Reapers battery pack and blew it up the armour would render itself inert. But said battery pack was about the size of a brick and sealed with titanium alloy. You needed to hit it just right and even then the charge might not be enough. And the fact that the battery was made of titanium alloy and wasn't magnetic posed a problem. It was a chink but not a possible weakness. They were working on it. Night and day.

Tyris's Reaper squad were back on the *Defiant* and the cruiser was orbiting Rygon Five. They were preparing in the next few weeks to do another Paradox run. This time twice the amount and twice the potency. They would double their money again. This time they would really line their pockets. And get state of the art weaponry. (not that they hadn't taken enough from the armoury in the Imperium.) But bullets cost money. Especially The splitter rounds that they seemed to prefer to any other. Tiris gathered a hundred thousand rounds of splitters with five hundred magazines. They were hard cocked and ready to rock with the ammo. They began to fill the magazines with fifty bullets in each magazine. Then they filled the various pockets with the magazines. Which was ten pockets in total. Per trooper. They were armed to the teeth, and nothing could bring them down, or so they thought.

The Trill were working on the weakness and the problem of the Medusa seed. They knew that if they could break down the toxin they would be half insured that the toxin was vulnerable and could be stopped. A Trill tech scientist was close to breaking the molecular structure of the Medusa Seed. And rendering it useless. He also had plans for a vaccine that would stop the molecular breakdown of the Trill. But these were in the early days of research. He was close to turning this war into the favour of the Trill. But still they worried about the Reapers. And the High King of the Trill was growing impatient. With more losses on the space front, it was looking like they had tough times ahead. Seeing as their energy weapons were of no use. This was because the Imperium had perfected and mass produced an organic damper. This was used to the maximum potential of the Troopers. And the standard K78 armour was rigged with the organic chip. That stopped the blue lightning charge, that made the weapons useless. The Trill had lost many of their soldiers. And thought the war was over. But the Trill high command insisted on them fighting with the old-fashioned way. Bullets, laser beams, Plasma cannons and of course high explosives.

Then came the Reapers and the Medusa seed. But still the Trill moved forward. That's when Tiris got sick of the Imperium, struck out a deal with the Trill. This would change the shape of the Faith Wars. And give the Trill a fair position with the Medusa seed. This he hoped would settle old scores, but the Trill were having trouble finding a vaccine and because of the way it left the Trill nothing but skin and genetic mess. In other word's it cooked the Trill inside out. Sending their bones and organs into goop, they looked on this with total horror. They thought they were finished as a race. But the

High King of the Trill wasn't giving up no he was just more provoked by the war seeing this obstacle as nothing but a minor challenge. He knew how smart his Tech heads were and they were becoming more and more clever, making weapons and defences against the Troopers.

They had become that little bit more Important in the grand scale of things, but things were becoming more-clear in how to stop the Medusa Seed. They were working day and night. And the solution was close to being discovered. And both The Emperor and the High King knew this. The war was growing old, with more Troopers and Trill soldiers mountain up as the death count was round about even. Tiris settled the debt with the Merchant and stowed the gold credits away on the *Defiant*. They had doubled their money again. They then decided to go back to Rygon see if they could get a little more smuggling work. And seeing as they had a knack for doing this, they had little need for encouragement. They had started out with nothing and now they were rolling in gold credits. At least four billion each. They were also the top mercenaries. Word had spread about the way they had destroyed the Meat Pirates, and that they hadn't even taken a scratch. This left them with a reputation for being immortal. And Tiris liked that. He even wallowed in it, this had kept things in perspective and knowing the Emperor he wouldn't like that and would send Reaper Team one out to find them and he knew that Alex Cardis would be on the hunt for them. He smiled to himself and wondered if the battle was worth it. Whether they would be better running. But that would only delay the inevitable. That's when they got a job smuggling slaves to the outer rim of the marches.

This was a new thing to Tiris but it paid extremely well. They would get six billion for the journey. And it would only take a couple of weeks. Tiris looked at the coordinates and punched them into the sat nav. They shot into space engaging the hyper drive as the crew kept the engines ticking over and clean. The *Defiant* had one of the best hyper drives Tiris had seen. He was proud of his new ship and also the *ESP*. The *ESP* in particular had proven its worth in the battle with the Meat Pirates. Tiris lit another cigar and smiled as he did so. He was fond of the reputation he had gathered onto himself and also Reaper team two. Nobody had the guts to short change Tiris and his squad of Reapers. But fate held fixed, and they were destined into a fight in which would either kill or make them the most deadly team of Storm troopers.

Alex arrived at Rygon Five. His team of Reapers and a hundred shock troops were in the Cruiser The *Brevity*, a huge battle cruiser, with enough fire power to split a small planet in two. Alex thought about serving the planet with Martial Law and seizing up the Paradox trade. Then getting the information he needed.

"Fuck it," He said, "Declare Martial Law".

The shock troops did their duty and rounded up the head dealers of the illicit drug Paradox. They then executed them. The rest of the population soon fell into line. The Paradox trade ground to a halt. As the orders were, seize and destroy the product. The Reapers kept everything in line. And the *Brevity* enforced the law. Just like a dog bearing its teeth. The populace of Rygon saw the danger and did as it was told. They even got information on the whereabouts of Tiris. Alex smiled as the dealer who had brokered the deal with Tiris spilled his guts, just before Alex blew a hole right through the addicts head.

A small Scout ship had managed to get away from Rygon Five, and was heading in the direction of Tiris. The pilot was one Kurt Lidel and him and his crew knew the value of credits all too well. And it was better to be friends with the devil than be his enemy, and Kurt was sure as hell that Tiris and his squad were more than a match for Reaper team one. He was very near positive of that fact. But still he would be better staying out of the battle that was looming over his head, he would though help by warning the *Defiant* about what lay in store at Rygon Five. He sent a communication to the *Defiant* "Code one, *Defiant* avoid returning to Rygon as Reaper squad one has declared Martial law on the planet and shut down the paradox shipping. I repeat Avoid at all costs, as they lie there waiting". The message hit about six hours later. And Tiris knew it was serious, he could tell by Kurt Lidel's voice.

Tiris and Kurt were old buddies both being Troopers in the same unit. Both having a severe distaste for the Imperium. And both watched each-others backs. Brothers in arms. They had calculated a strategy first chance they got. And that strategy was to render the Empire inert, useless. But these things were easier planned than executed. But Tiris had fulfilled his part by selling the Medusa seed to the Trill. Kurt was a Back-up man to him and his crew watched from different vantage points. This enabled Tiris to breathe and be cautious at the same time. Nothing surprised Kurt and nothing went by Kurt. He had often been the saviour of Tiris, who had often left a large stash of gold credits in certain stations with the key code being transmitted to Kurt. This had accumulated into a very large pot of gold. Kurt knew his place and never let Tiris down. They even managed to meet up and drink a cask of ale. The two of them howling into the cosmos. They had remained friends since the beginning of the Faith Wars. Where they had made a blood oath to carry on with their sabotage. They even sealed it in blood, two of them bandaged arm to arm. They had done this a short while before Tiris was suited with the K11 armour and given the Reaper Squad two to command. He smiled and sent a com link back to Kurt.

"Thank you Kurt We will take it under advisement". He then switched off the communications. Set his Cruiser to go dark. This meant, the ship was quiet and no one could make a sound as they sidled past the Rygon galaxy. Not tripping any radar traps. That he knew would be set by the Reaper team one. Sleeping satellites. That sent of a pulse to Alex on the *Berevity*. They headed for the Trill area of the Marches. Where they would sidle down into a stasis, a nice bit of peace, this would be much needed break for the Reaper Team. They would stay afloat just outside the Trill's home world. Carinthian. It was the only thing that seemed to settle Tiris, he didn't see it as treachery no he saw it as survival. That and there was a fat profit in the selling of Imperium secrets. He had sent codes and everything, ways to get past the energy shields that surrounded most of the Imperium's home worlds. These and other secrets that only a high military rank could access.

Tiris was now the most wanted man in the universe, Fifteen billion gold credits for him alive and Twenty-five dead. The rest of the reapers were a million dead or alive, but the shock troops who were scanning the cosmos, knew that it was unlikely to hand them over alive. The armour really was that good. Tiris sent a communication to the Trill home-world.

"Carinthian We are here to trade."

The world and its many space ports who were filling up war cruisers with Trill soldiers. Sent a communication back. "Yes Colonel, just in the nick of time".

Tiris smiled and switched the *Defiant* onto auto pilot and said, "This set of codes is just what you need to bring the Empire to its knees."

The auto pilot took them into a grav field that docked the *Defiant* very gently. Tiris smiled as the ships docking doors hissed as they opened and Reaper Team two walked onto what use to be their enemy's, home world. Tiris enquired about Cascoe, Who had departed in the early hours of that morning spearheading the attack. Him and his crew had been inoculated with the Medusa seeds anti toxin, it had just made it out their tech labs and Cascoe had been adamant about being the first ones with the inoculation. He had very little patience these days and the first sign of a breakthrough he put him and his crew first to test the antidote. That had made him first to attack the Imperium. He was privileged and honoured in this task. He had made himself a frontline Guinea Pig but this made him smile. This was how he had envisioned it the first of the Trill to stop this war, and hopefully win it in favour of them. But this was not a walk in the park, nothing this bloody and thought out was simple. No it was complicated and you rode the massive ion storm with bloodied and tight knuckles. A split second and you could be dead, ripped apart by machine conjured weapons. Cascoe wasn't scared, no, in fact he was quite enamoured by this being the last assault, the last charge of the Trill. He was still sure that if it did end in death. That him and his crew on the war cruiser would have died honourably. The Trill who was overseeing the Reaper squads payment in gold credits smiled through his whiskers. Showing his vampire like fangs said, "You know you are one of the Trill saviours".

Tiris smiled and placed his skull over his head. Then locked and pressed the com link on his wrist, "right lads we are no longer under obligation".

The squad smiled as Tiris went to the helm of the *Defiant*. They wanted little else other than some freedom and they knew just the place to go and live for a number of years. Orion the system that the Faith Wars had got its name from the battlefield where the Imperium had lost at least half its Storm Troopers. In the first few days. This was due to the Trill's deadly blue lightning weapons. The weapon caused the human Troopers, organs to implode and the troopers were hard at that fact. Then a couple of years later the Linsani planets had come up with a way to stop the impact of the Trills weapon. It was a Bio tech chip that was implanted on each of the Trooper. This was also the time that the Medusa Seed nerve toxin had first been used. And the way of war turned into the Imperium's favour. Then came the new K11 armour but it was over a million credits per suit and They erred on the side of caution and made two squads, reaper team one, headed up by Alex Cardis. And reaper team two, Tiris Cord. They headed deep into the Orion system. That was a grave yard of battlecruisers. And Trill warcrafts. But this didn't bother Tiris as he had been one of the lucky few to survive. The onslaught.

Chapter Seven

They headed to the space station Orgis two. A small space station that housed renegade Troopers and Pirates. They were safe there as it was too obvious to everyone that deserters would make camp in one of the Marches most obvious places. But this was just a lay low tactic for Tiris, he would refuel and sell some Paradox product. Then he would head further into the Orion galaxy, looking for a decent tech world, one of about nine to eleven. They arrived at the space station and were immediately greeted with howls of cheering and laughter. They stepped into the crowds as it made them feel special. They knew they had struck a blow for all mankind. The majority of the race thought they should never be at war in the first place. This was only shown as the dead and destroyed tombs of ships with floating decaying bodies were everywhere. If anything it would make the fight equal and fair.

They were heroes, and the destruction of the Meat Pirates had been noticed as well. They were happy to find that their fortunes were not too ominous. They had done the right thing in dealing with the Trill and the meat heads well that was fun. They also found that people in this system were helpful and not just for money no. They were taken for proper heroes, worshipped and emulated in the radio waves and television. They had made a lot of sweet friends in this abysmal no holds barred war with the Trill. Both sides had taken massive losses and there were rumours that even the Emperor wasn't safe with what the Trill had in store. That's why they knew they were not likely to be betrayed in this quadrant of space. It held many secrets and knew nothing was hard and fast. Nobody betrayed nobody and things were done in the proper manner. With respect and dignity. Reaper team two was held as the new age of order and would make its name as a force that even the Imperium would hail as truly triumphant.

That's right Tiris held one hell of a hand. He was holding the codes to the Troopers armoury, which was rumoured to have seven or eight more Reaper suits. But this would have to wait as the Trill wanted blood and blood was all that would satiate their souls, They were heading straight from past the Milky Way and straight to Terrar the home world of The Emperor. Cascoe was in his Warcraft and was briming with confidence as he and several smaller craft around his, all ready to defend as Cascoe landed his troops, first on the space station Teren. Then the rest would be deployed on the mother world Terrar. Cascoe would stay until they entered the Imperium stronghold Becrest. Then he would join the fight. But only once they made sure they had secured the Becrest Stronghold. The Troopers put up a bloody fight especially when they saw their Medusa seed was inert. And the Trill were surviving and attacking with Plasma cannons and laser rifles and wicked semi-automatic carbines.

The Troopers did all they could to keep the Trill at bay. But facts were facts, the Trill were unbeatable.

Especially seeing as they had turned the Faith Wars back around. And that the Emperor himself shot himself with a bullet. And blew the back of his skull against the throne. He did as he couldn't bear the thought of what the Trill would do to him. Cascoe got to the Emperor's Throne room with little resistance. He had to see the corpse of such a worthy opponent, he was a mortal enemy of the Trill and deserved the option of suicide, that which he took. Cascoe smiled knowing that he would have died in two days anyway.

They had an infiltrator who had been slowly poisoning the Emperor. With a Trill substance that was only lethal in small doses that mounted up, the rest of the servants took his pallid and weak nature to be his addiction to Paradox. Cascoe smiled as he looked upon the throne with blood and skull at the back of the Emperors slumped head. The brains he had were smattered and cauterised. He had fired a splitter into his head. This had done the damage and done the damage well.

Cascoe punched in the codes that Tiris had given to the Trill they were to stop the self-destruct setting, that was immediately turned on as the Emperor was no fool, he would take the Becrest with him. Cascoe smiled through his feline vampire like teeth.

"And that is that," he said as he switched the code red alarm off.

They were truly the winners. The rest of the Trill warlords were on route to the Terrar worlds where they would gather as many troopers as they could, and decide their fate later on. Probably round them up and set a massive nuclear detonator to vaporise the whole Trooper army. But this was easier said than done.

The Troopers were always loyal and the ones that weren't, gave up and sought immunity. The Faith Wars were drawing to the end. With the Trill being the better hunter. Tiris watched the destruction of the armies of the Imperium. He even toasted the Generals as they were executed on the spot and beheaded. A row of severed heads lined each side of the Becrests pathway into the large metallic fortress. The Trill sensing their victory, didn't make light work of it. They immediately got to work changing the codes and letting the war cruisers into Terra's Orbit.

Cascoe was immediately contacted by the Trills High King. He complemented the Trill warlord and guaranteed him anything he asked. Cascoe spoke to the king with much amusement. The king was about to enter a new age where the Trill were masters of the Universe. The Empire dead and wasted. He also sent a small Trill Scout ship to find the *Defiant*. On board was six billion gold credits and a personal thank you message to Tiris. Cascoe smiled at this as the other Reaper team were at Rygon waiting for Tiris and his ship the *Defiant*. They would have a long wait, as Tiris had overshot the Regis system and was in the war desecrated system of Orion. The *Defiant* had made to the centre-point, and sat back and watched as the Trill won the Faith Wars. They had survived.

Chapter Eight

Alex Cardis and his team of reapers were suddenly aware that the war was over and that the Empire had lost. He sat down bewildered by the sure magnitude of the Faith Wars and now it seemed like they had lost and had no one to call master. No one to tell them what to do, But Alex knew that they had been betrayed by the Reaper team two. He growled as he got up and walked to the console of the *Berevity*.

"Right Lads I know you think this is over but I have a score to settle and I intend to settle it do or die."

The lads, all ten signed on to the *Berevity*. Clockland, Erris, Tasdan, Cantor, Sidle, Cartmin, Duster, Render, Apolix, and Notsfur. Cardis smiled as he knew each of the Troopers were loyal. And he was short of nothing, if not nerve and he was positive that he would end the other Reaper team. But finding the team was another matter. He smiled, they could be in the deep folds of space. Or travelling lightly to the ends of the milky way. Then it dawned on Alex. "He's holed up in the Orion system" he said, then began to search for the star maps of the system.

He looked at said charts and scrolled down to the nearest space station that was open to trade. "Orgis two," said, Alex.

That was a week's journey away, he smiled and took off his helmet. And set his power armour onto charge. The rest of Reaper team one, followed suit. They then sped off to the Orion nebula. The eleven in the reaper team relaxed, as they knew it was going to be a hard fight with each team having the same Power Armour and the same weapons, but they both knew it was going to be a slug fest. With each of them being of equal strength and knowing their opponent was practically invulnerable, it would take this fight right down to brass tacks. Power fists and using their cunning and guile.

The ship sped off to the Orion system. Where Tiris lay in wait. He knew that Reaper team one was hunting them and it was only matter of days before they would descend upon them, Tiris smiled, he could make it to the Imperium armoury that was on a world called Emporium Bizarre. It was where Tiris had acquired the Medusa Seed and it was also the armoury of the human race. They started to settle into a nice restful pace and hoped they wouldn't have much time to waste. Just as they arrived at the imperialist armoury, The Reaper team one was arriving at Orgis two. The two of them, missing each other by mere hours. The *Berevity* looming over the small space station Orgis two. Tiris entered the security code for the armoury on its outer beacon, letting them pass through into the Armoury's cache. They entered and went straight to the Power Armour K11 top of the range. There were eight spare suits, and they also helped themselves to state-of-the art Laser rifles and Plasma cannons. They then they helped themselves to some incendiary rounds for their carbines, them and more splitters. They then found a few things for the *ESP.* More tactical nuclear missiles (Sidewinders) and space mines that would blow the biggest of ships to pieces. They also gathered several boxes of smoke and fragment grenades. They even gathered some nuclear detonators. Enough to see them on their way. And enough to take the fight to Cardis and his Team, Reaper one.

"What do you think lads, engage or evade?" The team smiled, all of them and Bucker replied, "Right lads were here for the species. Answer your superior".

They all laughed then spoke with surety, "Engage Sir!".

Tiris looked at his new stogie and responded, "Good I'm tired of this chicken shit running away" They all strapped themselves in whilst the crew began to put the *Defiant* into full throttle. Tiris sat back and looked grim, he knew this would be a very tough battle. The ship purged itself then fired through. Taking the team of reapers into the Orion nebula. They then headed for Orgis two. This was going to be a stand-up fight. And Tiris knew this, he had wondered since the day he put on his K11 armour whether it would come up and be useful or would they just trade blows forever. Until one of them mastered the fight and got the upper hand.

This was a feeling of anxiety for Tiris, as he knew that the Reaper team one had the upper hand if it came down to a battleship fight. They had the larger cruiser and more men, with at least 100 shock troopers. They were all armed to the teeth and the armour was decent enough for them to go suicide with a large amount of explosives. They were trained and trained well, But the K78 armour was not able to withstand the might of the Reaper team two. They came into proximity of the

Space station and could see the *Berevity* docked onto the years old Orgis two. They were laying down the law asking questions about the *Defiant*, and its crew. They were making sure that the station would not hold Tiris in its favour. They were maiming and killing anyone who didn't have a clue as to where the *Defiant* was. The ones who did as they were told, well they got fired out the air lock, into zero gravity where they were turned into mush, this was the price of turning on their own, it was seen as more a punishment. They would be better keeping silent. It was a shit deal either way. But necessary. The captain Alex Cardis was now in control of *Orgis two*. Just as The *Defiant* arrived Cardis was throwing out the Stations Leader into the dark murky abyss that was space. His veins exploded as he gasped for air. His muscles twisted and contorted and his bones couldn't sustain the pressure. He was ripped and torn to pieces. He Would have been better to keep silent. As that was pain that no man could sustain. Alex saw the *Defiant* drawing near to the station, he smiled and switched on the comm link.

"Okay Tiris how do you want to play this?" He asked/

Tiris stared at the nearby area and saw at least twelve bodies ripped apart. He growled and told his men to stand by.

Tiris flipped his comm link on and said, "We'll be right there Alex" They then docked and readied themselves. The two at the front with Plasma cannons. They were Cauldwell and Piper, they were ready for anything Dayton was next and he was surrounded by Spider mines. He was also ready for anything. The rest as-well as Tiris carried on into the stations main deck.

Cauldwell and Piper got through to the mess deck when they came under fire from some of the *Berevity's* shock troopers. They were firing at the two plasma cannon holding Reapers who were again laughing, they gave them a second to reload then they fired the huge energy weapons at them, making a hole in at least three of them at a time. They stopped as the shock troopers began to dwindle in numbers. Then Dayton passed along the corridor with about sixty spider mines. Cualdwell and Piper went to the rear as most of the damage was done. They flipped the switch and set their plasma cannons onto charge. This would take forty-five minutes. Then they would be back on point. Dayton carried on with each of the spider mines crawling onto one of the shock troops and then bang the things blew them to bits. The armour they were wearing wasn't powerful enough to withstand the incendiary and fragment charge that the spider mines carried. There were twelve or so left and Tiris told Dayton to stand down and cover the rear. Then it came to the crunch and all the shock troops were dead. They had only a few minutes to wait before Reaper team One made it to them. Tiris Had his Carbine cocked and ready to rock. He loaded a fresh magazine, splitters. He was confident in his grip of the mini sub machine gun. As were the rest of his squad. They were all ready to make Reaper team one non-existent. But this was easier said than done. They would have to throw everything that they had at them whilst they flung everything they had at them. It was going to be messy. Then after that it would be with the skill of the dagger and fist. As the power armour was so strong that it could take every-thing they both had. And I do mean everything.

Alex lifted his skull like helmet and put it on and switched his armour onto full power. The rest of his squad did the same. They then locked and loaded, and started to walk towards the other Reaper team. Tiris Cord produced a wicked knife, the edge was laser sharpened and balanced well for throwing. He was fully trained in the martial arts and had done specialist training with the suit. So had Alex, this was when they had truly met each other and no they didn't have any common ground, in fact they were very jealous and bitter of each other. The Emperor had to keep them both on a short leash. Tiris had been itching for this day to come a day where they could see who the better Trooper was. Who had the most skill, and who was the best. It was going to be a bitter fight with no rules.

Tiris smiled and said, "Ready lads".

The squad aimed at the bridge direction, knowing that in a few seconds they would be in a fight for their lives. The Plasma gunners were just about finished in charging their weapons. The door slid open and Tiris aimed deep into the room. Then the first wave of weapons went off. The armour doing what it was suppose-to do and that was deflect and dampen down the energy weapons. Tiris threw in a small grenade a smoker. That covered him as went forth into the bridge deck, and he was fast upon Alex, throwing his dagger at the battle-hardened Alex. It struck and struck well, into the man's chest plate. It only caused minimal damage but Tiris knew a thing or two about the armour and it had an engineering flaw on the chest. Then Dayton sent one of his spider mines crawling up the Colonel's leg and settling on his chest right next to the dagger.

Boom and a lurch as the space station momentarily knocked itself off its axis. The charge had wrecked over half of Alex's K11 armour. And he was down on the ground. The dagger had done the trick. But that was a one in a million shot. And Tiris was not finished. He sprayed Alex's body with splitters. The body jerked and convulsed as the splitters did the damage.

"Nobody said it was fair," he said over the comm link to both his troops and the Squad of Reaper one, who came to halt and both sides stopped fighting. Reaper team one raised their hands and said. "Sorry sir".

It was the done thing between Troopers, If your superior was killed in combat then you surrendered. Knowing that a court martial was a walk in the park compared to going down in the heat of battle. And seeing as Tiris had discovered a chink in the power armour, they thought better of it than to try and fight, or they would end up the same way as their colonel. Tiris retrieved his dagger and stomped right on the dead officer, smashing his helmet and skull.

Tiris called Bucker to his side. The battle-hardened sergeant walked with Tiris, and Tiris removed his skull then lit another Stogie. He clipped the helmet onto the clip on the left-hand side of his hip. The helmet powered down and closed its AI. Tiris walked through to the *Defiant* enjoying his victory. The rest of Reaper two followed suit. He flipped his wrist comm on and spoke to Reaper team one.

"You are free of all duties in the service of the Imperium. You have two choices". The reaper teams both smiled at the compassion that had become second nature to Tiris. "You can join my squad and be under my command, or you can surrender your armour and live a life as a scout?"

All the Reaper team one decided to join Tiris and the Reaper team two. They saluted then shook hands with Tiris as they began to board the *Defiant*. Bucker smiled at the Troopers as they went by.

"What do we do with the Berevity?" asked Bucker.

Tiris lifted his finger to his comm link waited as the last of Reaper team one went by. "Scuttle her and smash her to junk." Tiris smiled and began to walk to the bridge. He got there and his crew were wondering what to do next. He smiled and punched in the coordinates for Rygon Five. He needed to see how much damage Alex had done to the Paradox flow. The systems where most of the narcotic was sold were crying out as they were on a forced cold Turkey, on a biblical scale. Addicts who didn't have any control of their habits were turning feral, dangerous. They were taken to cannibalism. And making home-made Paradox out of waste materials that had been used storing and fixing the drug. Like breaking up the roaches in a hashish den. They would be there in two weeks. And hopefully the Reaper Team one hadn't done too decent a job. Hopefully, they could re-construct the pipe lines to the various systems that they were reliant on. They traversed through space and headed to Rygon on the way they were joined by Kurt Lidel, who opened up the comm link to the *Defiant*.

"Hey Tiris, you're in one piece".

Tiris smiled and responded, "That fight was going only one way Kurt".

Kurt smiled and said, "I take it you figured out a chink in the K11 armour".

Tiris laughed a little and said, "It was on the cards. I had been over and over the armour and it dawned on me. Home is where the heart is and well the heart is on the chest, and a dagger in the heart and pulse monitor would weaken it enough to allow an explosive to destroy the suit and disrupt the power shield."

Kurt laughed, "Boy am I glad I aint your enemy".

Tiris smiled at this, "I take it you want to board Kurt and have a few drinks?"

Kurt laughed again, "Yeah man I'd love to howl at the stars with you".

Chapter Nine

Whilst this was happening, a new player in the Paradox trade was emerging. His name was Marcus and he had a fierce hunger to be number one bad guy in the Marches. He was a power hungry, leader. He commanded a fleet of seven destroyers and was known for his long hauls with the dangerously potent type of Paradox. It lived up to its reputation and was totally high risk when it was used for combat effectiveness. It was undefeated, I mean his shock troops where breathing in the stuff constantly, and it turned them into invulnerable maniacs. They could get peppered with explosive shredders (Shot gun ammo) and still have the energy to fight until their last breath. They were undefeated in the Marches. They were fond of beheading their enemies and setting them as a symbol.

Tiris had come up against Marcus when he was a young private, in the Imperium. And knew then that the Pirates he had were in vast numbers. They weren't reckless like the Meat Pirates, no these were hard core, using every tool of war to engage with the enemy, using surprise, hit and run tactics where they could. Was a means to an ends. But they had been in deep space for a long time, since before the Reapers had been on the scene, and they were greeted with howls of joy as the Trill celebrated their victory over the Emperor and his Fascist regime.

Marcus smiled as he watched the Trill warlords celebrate their victory. He got a buzz from the fact that he could now go back to his conquest of the Paradox narcotic. And trade was going to be good as he now had one less authority to avoid. They arrived at Rygon Five and discovered that the Imperium had left its mark on the system. It had disrupted the drugs trade and supply. No, he knew though that it could be pulled back to a thriving trade. And supply and demand. Well his troops were a crack elite of serious Paradox Junkies. Who held no fear but needed to live on the narcotic. It was expensive to each troop. And you had to work for your fix. If Marcus, or one of his level headed generals said jump, you asked how high, just to make sure you heard him right. No, high times were going their way. He smiled as the last of the destroyers joined him at Rygon Five. Where they could pick up a good supply of the narcotic. But they would have to wait as the supply trade and produce was defunct after Reaper Team one had declared martial law and rounded up all the head dealers and blasted them. No this was going to take a while to secure a safe way to produce the drug especially in the amounts that Marcus needed and of course it had to be pure. Class A chip.

Kurt and Tiris celebrated their new found release. They were now under their own rules. And Tiris, well he was proud of that fact, he looked at Kurt with a smile and a happiness that he couldn't disguise and he had no need to. He then got an idea, 'Give Kurt a K11 suit of armour'. Kurt smiled and said, "If that doesn't makes us true brothers then nothing will". Tiris who was slightly drunk smiled and the two of them headed for the cargo hold were the armour was situated. He opened, the power armour cargo box that the titanium alloy power armour was in and handed him the helmet first, The creamy bone coloured Skull was AI initiated and had a targeting guided laser scanner that showed the best offensive actions. He then began to push the rest of the armour onto his body. The grav field cushioned and made the armour feather lite. The skull helmet rested comfy on his shoulders as the AI lit up and caused slight disorientation. Kurt smiled to himself and thought 'So this is what Immortality feels like.'

Tiris shook the bone exo-skeleton hand that fitted like a glove. The AI patched him up with the rest of the Reaper teams. "Reaper teams one and two sound off so as Kurt can get to know you. "Dayton", "Artemis", "Cauldwell", "Crassent", "Piper", "Armstrong", "Hue", "Samster", "Bucker", "Pleasence". Tiris smiled and then shouted for the reaper team one to sound off, "Cloakland", "Erris", "Tasdan", "Cantor", "Sidle" "Cartmin", "Duster", "Render," "Apolix," "Notsfur", "And yourself", "Lidel" He said. They then bedded down for the night, well for an eight-hour sleep cycle.

Marcus called his lieutenant and his rearguard sergeant, The Lieutenant 'Grimsford' was a tall skinny and very bony man with a constant shaved head, and also sporting his scars that he had gained in battle. On his face and hands mainly. Nicks and cuts from being at the tail end of fragment grenades, His body was peppered with Buck shot weapons. Many an enemy had thought him dead but he was playing possum. Then he would strike with a wicked bowie knife. Then vanish into the mists of war. He could play that game of mouse and cat all day, all night, all week. The guard sergeant was a broad but deceptively tall. He had managed to postulate himself so they would be enemy would think him weak and frail. This was all done with meditation and ancient Ninja Yoga. He was dressed all in black with age old K78 armour, half of which was in dire need of repair. But he knew that it was all the protection he needed. He had sent many an enemy to the icy cold vastness of space. He loved to send his crack unit of Paradox hungry mad men into battle. Like I said they never lost. Marcus smiled and faced the two men. "We need to get the Paradox flowing again". Said Marcus. To the rearguard sergeant he looked most Gravely at Coljax, who stood with a dour look on his face, he was impassive to everything accept the leaders voice. Marcus pulled his mask that was always pumping Paradox. And began to inhale and breathe the toxic narcotic.

The *Defiant* picked up the signals of the Pirates surrounding the Paradox home world. Tiris moved to the bridge after he was summoned by the leader of his flight crew.

"Sir?"

Tiris roused himself, "what is it son?"

The chief engineer breathed and said, "Sir, I think we should go elsewhere".

Tiris pushed his armour back on and replied, "Why, what seems to be the problem?"

"Pirates, sir".

Tiris pulled up the monitor in his quarters and looked at the seven destroyers as they stayed in orbit. "If that's who i think it is then we've got trouble".

"Well push us by the Paradox crazed Pirates".

The head of engineering was first to hit the cloaking device that the *Defiant* had newly acquired. The *ESP* was also fitted with one. And Bucker was told to pass by with the *ESP* under his command. Lidel then departed in his new armour and decided to send the Pirates on a misdirection. He would shoot past Rygon Five and head for the outer rim of the marches. He closed all forms of transmission so it seemed like he was blind and for some reason running away. But Tiris and the *Defiant* sidled passed immune to all forms of tracking. Bucker and the *ESP* followed closely behind shielded with their cloaking devices. But Kurt wasn't taking any chances and thrust straight by with what looked like to be a Naval Flagship behind it, this was made by a satellite giving off a strong Pulse which gave off the impression that it was a Naval battlecruiser and was hot on the heels of Kurt Lidel.

He had done this several times to help out various scouts and world engineers. It was called party planning and cost a tidy amount of gold credits. He never missed with that trick. And as usual the aggrieved party didn't know what to make of the satellites pulse. They usually got out the way. Knowing that something that big was trouble. But it was an illusion and no one thought to find out if it was a trick. No one had the guts to stay around to watch. Knowing naval destroyers are usually armed to the teeth. And anything going that fast was obviously in trouble with either the Trill or the Imperium. And Kurt he didn't give a fuck. He was head over heels with his new armour. He would catch up with Tiris later and they always made sure that they stayed in contact. He was always around in case things got too hairy for Tiris and Tiris always paid well.

The *Defiant* pushed through quietly and headed for the furthest away star port. That was an old, abandoned Naval star port called Sigmus Twelve.

They would Dock there and wait for movement away from Rygon Five. It was now being used as a smuggling den. And a port to call fellow deserters, and find tracks to new places to go. Places that were held dear by the likes of Tiris, and Kurt. It was the first place that the Trill warlord had met Tiris, just shortly after Tiris got his armour. And Kurt introduced them. It was a different place now as they were all partying and celebrating their new found freedom. It was a joyous time and nothing smelled as sweet when the tyrant was beheaded and a new universal order was claimed by the Trill and the tired and decrepit relics of the Imperium were decaying and losing all hope.

Tiris never thought anything of it as he had done what over half of the Troopers had been contemplating. They knew why as-well. The Emperor was a total tyrant, one of the most cold and sinister men to run the known Universe. He had been cruel since the day he could talk, his favourite pastimes were making the servants uncomfortable, sneaking up, breathing the air with sinister connotations. And occasionally as he grew older he began to use and abuse his privileges, raping and murdering certain servants. Everybody knew he was a psychotic maniac and he ran the empire in a total state of fear.

Tiris smiled as the docking procedure ran its course. They then boarded the star port and went straight to the main deck where they were greeted by a whole host of people, most people had heard rumours about the reaper teams, but few had seen them and even fewer had seen them in action. The rumours were true, they were the exact face of death. And no one could even halt them. They were invulnerable, unstoppable and always exacting in their trade and that trade was death. They had made the myths true. They each looked like the Grimm reaper and the armour was impenetrable.

One smuggler said to his friend, "They say the last thing you hear when a reaper is on you is the dry laughter of death himself."

They looked on in awe as the crème da la crème walked past. Tiris went through first then the rest of the two reaper teams decided to relax and stood at ease as Tiris met up with the Stations commander. The two men gripped wrists and made haste, with the war being over they both could relax, the commander Arteris smiled and let go of his wrist.

"You okay Tiris?" came the question from Arteris.

Tiris sniffed and said, "Yeah I'm fine, thank fuck the Faith Wars are over huh".

Arteris smiled at the Colonel and poured him and Tiris a glass of wine. Then the star ports commander asked the six million gold credits question, "Why are you here?"

Tiris placed his glass down and replied, "I'm here because I can't go to Rygon Five as it is swarming with Paradox Pirates". Arteris drank some more wine then responded, "Ah Marcus and his henchmen Grimsford and Coljax. They will be busy trying to restart the paradox trade routes".

Tiris smiled and replied, "well more power to them".

Arteris put down his glass as-well, "Well its gonna take some time and of course they will want to use this station as a stash and smuggling port".

Tiris smiled and hooked his helmet onto the side of his hip. He then joined the rest of his crew and began to celebrate. This was a god send of course as none of them had been able to relax since they had deserted. And that was many cycles away in the past, Tiris sat down and lite up a stogie. Then drank some beer. The reapers were lapping up their freedom. No more Imperium, no more death squad reapers, no they were set for life. Especially after giving the Trill the genetic code for the medusa seed. Now they would wait and party for a while. Then when the going was good they would depart from Sigmus Twelve and carry on smuggling and trading until there was no need for them to be around. Then they would retire and live up the life of a king each of them. Each one knowing only the might of the Faith Wars was finished. And now the trill was in command. They had no purpose. No things were looking brighter for the two reaper teams.

Chapter Ten

Whilst the Storm troopers celebrated, the Linsani home world was having a major crisis in its research and biological development. They had been on the verge of making a super soldier with DNA and chemical bonding to produce one of the most lethal bugs that could be controlled and sent into the forefront of wars and would accumulate the most casualties. They had been on the verge for some time and knew that they were close to a prototype. An extremely lethal super bug with dark, bone dense matter that shielded its heart and head. It also had large talons that could tear through the hull of most large battlecruisers. Then they boarded the ship and began to tear apart the Troopers with an insane appetite for destruction.

The programme for the research into Dark Talon one was just about to finish when everything went haywire. The station in the Orbit of Linsani's world was torn asunder by the Dark Talon the monster it turned out to be was too much and it had escaped and released the rest of the Dark Talons. A number of sixteen of them, each hungry and desiring nothing more than chaos and destruction. They enjoyed the raw power that it gave them when they were let of the leash. But this was more permanent and they were free to create merry Hell on whomever came into contact with them. They shut down the station and carried on their feeding frenzy with the human inhabitants. You could hear the screams and bone sickening crunch as the ripped apart the Linsani scientists. The blood was everywhere. The parts of the scientists were strewn all over the space station. Guts and the rancid smell of guts and organs was everywhere. The scientists that had managed to escape on the stations skiffs were immediately picked up and taken to safety. This was only sheer luck and desperate measures that had got them to the three man skiffs that there was seven of. One of them never made it from the lock. It was grabbed by two of the dark Talons and ripped apart. Then, well the carnage had really begun, the three scientists were torn apart and devoured by the Dark Talon.

Tiris sat on his bed and began to add up how much profit they had, it was a tidy sum and they had made a nice comfortable profit. The ship didn't cost too much and it was cheap to run and they had enough ammunition to carry them into a new war. That's when they got the distress call from the Linsani space station. The crew of the *Defiant* were wary of the call but then the images of the destruction were sent through to them. The corpses, what was left was shown as total carnage. Tiris spoke into the comm link to all the Reapers and two the engineering crew. "One of the Emperors pets has got loose, anyone want to go on a bug hunt?"

Each of the reapers sounded off.

Then Bucker spoke, "What's in it for us?"

Tiris smiled and replied, "I have no idea but if its good enough we'll take it". He then proceeded to get in contact with the Linsani worlds authorities. He waited for the response. "Five billion," came the response. Tiris smiled through his helmet. "Five billion," he said into the comm link to the two squads of reapers.

Bucker sighed and went, "That's a bit much, make sure you get all the bugs data sir".

Tiris smiled again, "Rodger that," he said. Then he opened up the data link between them and the Linsani system. "We'll be there in a week, send me the data on the bug".

They then began their journey to the Linsani worlds, Tiris glanced at the screen with the words Dark Talon on it. He began to read, an exceptional warrior bug, the dark Talon was a new way to conquer whole planets. They had ways to keep the bug restrained, only that these ways were becoming more and more useless. And they were having to come up with more new methods, methods that were becoming more and more useless. Then well, well they got the shock of their lives as the Dark talons shook off their restraints and escaped.

Tiris read more and more, realizing that this was only a matter of time until they shook their shackles and destroyed their masters. As for how much damage it would take to kill one of them. It was very near impossible. As the exo-skeleton that covered it's chest and head was so dense, that only a direct hit from a plasma cannon would kill it, And even that wasn't a certainty. He carried on reading looking for weakness, in particular, hand to hand, He realized that these things were super enhanced and totally bred for war. Then came its strengths, it had super human strength and lack of oxygen wasn't a problem, it didn't breathe air. And had the strength thirty or so men, that was how it managed to rip open hulls of battlecruisers. Then they would decimate the entire crew and Troopers being as they were indestructible. And let's face it, the Dark Talon project was still hush hush. Giving it the element of surprise.

But the fight that Tiris was going to have was a tough one, And seeing as the Dark Talon project had no weaknesses and the Reapers had the K11 armour it was difficult to see who would win. He kept on studying the data that was the Dark Talon project. The closest to a weakness he could find was under the left armpit, but with its strength and mobility it was very near impossible to get the weakness. But Tiris knew that they would have get close to them so as to do any damage at all. Tiris sent everyone in the reaper squads the weakness and told them that they were going to have to get hands on, bloody and brutal. "And boys watch their claws".

He then sent all the data on the Dark Talons to the Reaper squads. To be fair the Talon and the Reaper squads were about equal, But the Talon were unconditional, and lacked the thought of dying as they were more insect than animal. If one died it was taken as food for the younglings. In fact the Dark Talon were taken to sacrificing itself to keep the species around and it was the only thing the species knew, it was programmed into them. Eat, kill and die, because most of them were on short life spans after reaching full on maturity. They often died just after their first combat term. They were black as scorpions and once fully matured they had the lethality of twenty or so Storm Troopers, but there was the problem, that they died a couple of months after reaching their peak of maturity and lethality. Then the younger Dark Talons would eat there dead it was a necessity to them and was part of their circle of life.

Most weapons dead end on impact, with the creatures exo-skeleton being harder than most of the steel hulls that they tore apart. They were slick black and looked just as sinister as the many life forms that were floating living in the Marches. But this was no subspecies no they were being bred for the destructive side of the Imperium. They had used the Dark Talon on several small skirmishes out with the Marches. They had travelled into the endzone of the Trill and used the Dark Talon to its full potential. Where they had unleashed the bugs on two warcraft battlecruiser's, The Trill didn't have a chance, as these bugs had been forced to starve especially when it came to the Trill. No the Linsani were always trying out weapons and chemical weapons, but the biological weapon Dark Talon was a ninety-nine per cent kill rate but they were having trouble keeping them on a leash.

In fact after releasing they couldn't be controlled. It was becoming a frequent problem. Then their holding pen, a station that was used by putting most of the Talon in carbon freeze. They then were slowly roused and sent into battle. But this time someone had sabotaged the whole station and started the whole stations carbon freeze to melt down and by the time they realised, the Talon had breached the holding pen cages and killed the few men that were watching the bugs. This had all been noted and taped on the AI that was part of the stations recording itinerary. It saw this figure deliberately sabotage the carbon freeze, the man crept in, went up to the main power panel and blew it up, sending the deep freeze out of action. The man then clambered out of the station and onto a small one man skiff, then flew away.

This was all caught on surveillance and the man was fast away. Tiris watched this all in calm resilience, the saboteur had made a good escape and was obviously pleased with his work. He circled the station in his skiff then flew off into the Emperor's controlled space. This was obviously a cold plan by one of the Imperium's so called friends. No in fact the war had finished so suddenly that the humans had nothing left to fight for except its own greedy selves. So things were naturally being removed from the Imperium accounts. Like Dark Talon, which if anyone asked about they were treated with silence and it was a deafening silence, usually before the cocking of a pistol and if you had time, a prayer. Tiris relaxed and watched the masked man who was obviously on paradox. But he was no usual mercenary, no, he had the swagger of a Storm trooper and a good one at that.

Bucker opened up the comm link and asked Tiris if he knew who that may be. "Sir he's a sniper from my old unit".

Tiris smiled of course, "Yes Bucker only your unit was axed about five years ago and how can you tell?"

Bucker clicked, "Well it aint his uniform, it's the way he walks. Only my unit have that calm stride with a sense of purpose".

Tiris watched the Saboteur a couple of times and hailed Bucker as sleep cycle was finishing. Bucker woke to his skull signalling him to make contact with Tiris. He put the skull on and sounded off. "Bucker here, what is it sir?"

Tiris breathed out, "Who was the man you were told to rear, who was like a son to you?"

Bucker quietly said, "Shit. That would be the young trooper who I busted out of my unit for unlawful killing".

Tiris knew he was digging up the past with Bucker, but knew that it needed to be broached, "Dascoe. Trooper Dascoe". Tiris snorted out and continued, "Didn't he make it out on a dishonourable discharge?"

Bucker nodded his head and said, "Yes he did Sir, did a stint in a Military prison. Then left and no one heard from him since".

Tiris was very near positive that that was his old student. And had been trained so well that only man who could stop him was Bucker. Bucker smiled as he watched the perfect precision of Dascoe he knew he would come into contact with him sooner or later. He had already tried to welcome him back into the fold of the Troopers. But the man had gotten greedy and wiped-out Buckers old unit and gotten a million gold credits a head. But he had made one definable mistake, he left Bucker alive. Bucker had been wary of his orders since. That had left him with the unmistakable urge to desert, that was when he met Tiris. They clicked instantly and Bucker felt secure under the command of Tiris. Then, and only then, did he feel as though he was doing the thing that was right. And the Imperium was getting too damn greedy. They had no respect for life, the Trill or the humans.

They had two more days until they were near the Linsani station. And well they didn't know what to expect. The station had been classed as off the grid. And no one and I mean no one was to set foot on the decrepit station. The *Defiant* closed in looking at the stations proximity. Bucker boarded the *ESP* and lit up the console and began to sweep the station with a life scan laser. That told him what life forms were on board, and whether they were human or xenomorph. There were no human life signs and one massive pulse of Xenomorph. Bucker flew the *ESP* back to the airlock on the *Defiant*

"It's hooching with xenomorphs sir".

Tiris snarled a little after watching the final transmission of the Linsani Dark Talon space station. They didn't stand a chance. Even if they had a little warning it still would have been too late. Dascoe had entered and successfully destroyed the Carbon Freezers and woke up a whole nest of Xenomorphs. What ensued was the destruction and eating of the inhabitants, including the technicians who had control over the Talons, and also the troopers that were there to insure the protection of the tech twelve experts. They were devoured, torn apart and didn't have a chance. No, all hope was lost to the Linsani tech team and also the Troopers they thought they would have been a match for the xenomorphs but the strength of them and their hunger was too much. For the garrison and the hundred or so Troopers. The *Defiant* then began a scan of the outer hulls and the skiff pods that hadn't made good their escape.

No they had been destroyed in and out with the three men in each ripped limb from limb. The blood splashing up the metallic walls and entrails of the tech's being left to decay in the cold reaches of space. The oxygen had been sucked right out of a huge gash on the hull of the station. Where they had exited and tore another gash in the rear of the station then entered the station and finished off the rest of the tech team and troopers. They were cold and methodical. The tech team, as well as the Troopers were finished and finished in a fashion that made Jack the Ripper look like a saint.

Tiris watched the carnage ensue and tried to figure what area to approach first. Should he settle for a two man strike team straight into the nest, or should he go into the station full throttle? He looked at the carnage as it ensued. Then decided best to head them full on and worry about their safety later. There was no need to rush things as they would be setting thermite charges and rolling them into the nest, these charges were high powered nuclear thermite that meant they could melt the Bones of most species. And I mean melt. Tiris readied the two squads to head into the station that was icing over and decaying, the bodies were everywhere, some were gnawed upon, some ripped apart and flung everywhere.

They began their sweep into the station, and quickly realised that not one single bug had been killed. That was not a good sign. Tiris smiled sadly into his skull. This was not going to be easy. In fact it was probably the most deadly bug that he had seen, this was plaguing his mind and sending him something that he had not felt since he was a raw recruit, fear, and he was no trainee recruit anymore, He had stood his ground numerous times and lost lots of brothers in arms. But this, this unnerved him and he was spooked.

Bucker on the other hand welcomed the feeling knowing that if he died, well he had lived well. Bucker took Reaper team one and made a sweep of the lower deck below where the Bugs had been kept in Carbon

Freeze. He smiled and set one of the Thermite charges onto the celling of the mess hall, directly below the nest. Reaper team two, were making progress into the bowels of the ship hoping they didn't rouse the bugs. They all smiled and got on with their jobs. They planted six thermite charges on and around the holding pen of the bugs. The plasma blast of each should melt at least half of the bugs the rest would have to take their chances in the cold, icy refines of space. By the time they knew what hit them they would be too late. They sounded off as the two squads finished their missions then headed carefully back to the *Defiant*. They had planted enough charges to nuke a small country.

"Releasing docking clamps," said Dayton. Then the door slid shut.

"Let's get the fuck out of here," said Tiris, who punched in the coordinates to one of the Linsani worlds, they had a bounty to pick up. Soon as they were a good distance away Tiris pushed the button on the charges. There was a bright flash and a loud ripple of noise. Then space dust circling around the station as it was melted and blown to bits. That was the end to the Dark Talon and its creators had one hell of a time covering it up.

Tiris removed the skull and carried on setting the coordinates to the Linsani home world Quadrant. This was where they would pick up six billion gold credits. Tiris assumed it was a job well done. But nothing that simple came easy, and the Linsani corporation was fond of keeping its secrets, well very secret, Tiris knew this well. What he didn't know was that certain fanatics of the old Imperium were planning a counter strike on the Trill using the Dark Talon's full capacity with several large carriers all heading to the Trills home world, where they would off load the dangerous Xenomorph and the fanatics would sit back and watch the desecration of the Trill. As they closed in on the Trill home world, they thought that the damage would be easy to sweep under the carpet. Kurt Lidel was on his recon of the Trill home world when he spotted three of the cargo freights who were heading straight to the orbit of the Trills home world. Kurt looked for markings on the cargo holds and spotted a crack of light in a dark and cold tomb, it was the markings of a troop carrier. He immediately tried to get hold of Tiris.

"Tiris. This is Kurt we have a situation about to happen on the Home world of the Trill. I say again a situation about to happen on the Trill home world".

Tiris got the message and replied, "Who and how many are there Kurt?"

Kurt breathed a sigh of relief, "It looks to me like at least half a dozen large freighters carrying what looks like troopers".

Tiris growled, "Are there any other markings aside the Troopers?"

Kurt looked again at the lead carriers hull and left side. "Yep it's got a Linsani logo".

Tiris breathed out a sigh of exhaustion. "It's the Linsani's new pet Kurt you're going to have to leave the quadrant and I mean now soldier".

Kurt pushed his skull onto its fitting and replied, "I will rendezvous in two sleep cycles" Kurt signed off and set his Scout ship to auto pilot and decided that it was best to get some rest.

Chapter Eleven

The Trill home world gathered its soldiers and put the weak and the young into hiding. Then the first wave hit, the growling and snarling and sheer mass of black exo-skeletons began to tear through the infantry ripping the cat-like people limb from limb, some of them stopping to devour a soldier every now and then. The ripping and tearing of flesh and fur made the majority of the Trill lose morale and they began to flee causing complete panic. They never knew what hit them. Their strength and agility was little use and the sheer ferociousness of the new bug was, well making light work of the Trill. Tiris watched from a very far distance, with Trill Home World Television broadcasting the battle.

"These things are going to wipe out, our race," came the reporters scared and tired voice. "The emperor is dead, but I guess he had plans". The voice was strained and broken. "This is the most catastrophic contingency plan ever". It continued, "I gave our forces a chance against the Medusa Seed, but this this is something else, something diabolical."

The signal turned to static and white out signal with the message 'be back soon.' If they survive the night these things, these dark Talons were practically invulnerable. Tiris opened up the communications channel and sent an urgent message to Cascoe, Tiris waited for a reply from the Trill warlord, who was overseeing the mighty Imperium's last days in control of the mass of space in ten Quadrants (practically the whole known Universe). He heard the comm link whistle then pop.

"Sir it's Tiris, he says its urgent."

Cascoe opened up a comm link and said, "Yes my friend?"

Came the question come statement. "Your home world is under attack Cascoe". Cascoe immediately opened up the Martial channel. Hearing nothing he thought 'is this a joke?' Then realised whoever it was had obviously taken down the digital AI and all its neighbouring equipment.

"Tiris," he said, "I owe you more than you could know".

Tiris grimaced and watched some more as the desolation of the Trill carried on. Cascoe then patched into the Local News Report and saw what was happening. "What the fuck." he said "All Battlecraft, we are being invaded by what apparently is a last-ditch attempt to restore the Empire in all its hellish glory, they are using a biological weapon Called the dark Talon."

Tiris sent the information that he had on the dark Talon. Cascoe thanked him again. Then the war cruisers were boarded and they headed straight for the Trill home world. It would take about a week to arrive back at the Trill home world and hopefully the High King and his advisors would have made it off the Home world. The *Defiant* also headed in the direction of the Trills home world. Hoping it could help in the exodus of the planet. They would have to be quick as the other ships were sending the deadly xenomorph down to key areas on the planet. These were strategically positioned in order to do maximum damage and leave no scope for survivors.

They had had this planned for nearly five years now and the ferocity of the bug was not to be underestimated. They were cold bloodied killing machines, and the Trill didn't have a chance. The High King and his councillors abandoned the planet during the first wave of bugs, heading to a moon located on the furthest position away from the Trill home world. The Trill were losing huge amounts of soldiers and average people, civilians if you like. These bugs were exacting in their attack and showed no mercy or quarter. In the fact that the creatures were unremorseful. No conscience, no fear. They were invulnerable. The *Defiant* arrived two days after the last wave of bugs swept through the home world of the Trill. They left nothing alive and the bug had swarmed en mass. It was bloody carnage. Only one thing was left to do and this wasn't a perfect solution, that was tactical nuclear, Armageddon. But they needed the full might of the Trill armada to see this through to its fullest potential. Even then they didn't know if the Imperium had more of these carriers and who they would target next. It was obviously a last ditch at the Trill to get the Empire back to its formative glory.

They were already planning a successor to the Emperors throne. His name was Taxus and he was a cold bloodied mad man, just as bad as his predecessor (if not worse). The *Defiant* arrived at the Trill home world just as the six carriers headed back into deep space. They had done their job. And needed to go back to the biological station to pick up more of the Dark Talon. Then they would start to finish of the rest of the home worlds of the Trill. Taxus was placed onto the throne of the Imperium. And he reinstated the war council. And began his campaign in the same spirit of the Faith Wars. This was done in the only way it could be done by sending more troopers to the galaxies that were at war with the Imperium.

As the *Defiant* arrived and scanned the world for survivors. But nothing was alive apart from the Bugs who were finishing off the carcasses of the Trill. Devouring, eating and savouring the bodies as they ate, Tiris growled at this a deep throaty growl, as if to say, 'You motherfuckers'.

He opened his comm-link to Cascoe. "Cascoe come back".

There was a little static then the warlord replied, "Yes Tiris". Tiris responded, "Well sir your too late".

Cascoe punched in the coordinates to his home world. Cascoe breathed out and said, "That bad Huh?"

Tiris responded. "Yes sir too late, you're going to have to nuke the full planet".

Cascoe listened and replied, "I have to wait for the rest of the armada to get here". Tiris nodded and thought, 'Make sure the job is done right', "How long is that going to take?"

Cascoe drilled his fingers on the steel console and answered after a brief pause. "A couple of days until we are at full strength, then a day or so until the tactical warheads warm up then its full on nuclear strike".

Tiris then said, "Are we needed or are you ready to go?"

Cascoe thought for a moment. "I'd rather catch up with you, if you don't mind?"

Tiris smiled and replied, "Not a problem Cascoe".

Cascoe carried on drilling his fingers on the console.

Tiris relaxed for a second knowing that he needed to see the Trill Warlord as much as he needed to see him. Such was the relationship with the two of them. They had come a long way since the Medusa Seed. But this was different they now had an entirely different war on their hands. It was Biological it was treacherous, as this type of bug had never been seen the xenomorph was advanced and could survive most weapons, the crew of the *Defiant* had already destroyed one nest, and knowing the Imperium they would have these nests of Xenomorphs dotted all over the known universe. They must have been working on these for decades, Tiris thought.

He hung around the Trills quadrant and told the rest of the Reaper teams that they may be needed, the Reaper teams sounded off then went back to at ease. They were playing dice and drinking moderately. That meant they only drank a little so as to keep themselves sober and ready.

"Cascoe is on his way to meet with us," the reaper Teams leaders went.

"Rodger that sir!" Then all they had to do was two sleep cycles and they would be meeting with the Warlord of the Trill.

Kurt got back in touch with Tiris, "Tiris you need me just holler".

Tiris knew that Kurt was handy in a fight and if needs be to retreat. He had tricks up his sleeve. Tricks like the one he used earlier. The sleeping satellite was another, making the appearance of an abandoned, desolate, deserted warcraft. Then the party would attempt to board thinking it was free for salvage. Then either it would explode or the Reaper teams would lay an ambush. Kurt was quite the strategist when it came to helping Tiris and the other Storm Troopers that had deserted the Imperium.

The ceremony of Taxus was well underway and the look on the new Emperor was of cold steel he was a famed Storm Trooper who had got a reputation for being cold, both with the enemy and his own Troopers. He didn't let shit slide, to put it bluntly. He was known for his tough and rough justice, especially on deserters, He was a middle aged gentleman who was about six foot two inches, scars all over his back from the first fight he was dropped into and it was known he was the only survivor of that drop. His whole squad had been decimated in the first few minutes against the Trill, this was before they had the Linsani's biological dampening chips. And the Trills weapons were working to mass desecration of the Storm Troopers. Some say that he had held his ground until they were dead, all of them, others say he made a deal with the enemy and bartered his soul for a new fresh day in the Faith Wars. It was never really discussed by his fellow Troopers as they couldn't look at the man as his eyes were like black holes boring straight through you, and that was when he liked you.

The Imperial coronation went on and nothing could stop this new madman from taking over, no he was next in line and only because of his cold killing style. He sat as the crown was put on him. The gold sceptre in his left hand and ceremonial pistol in the other. This pistol was used to full effect on the mutinous and deserters that were caught. This had happened on a daily basis and just that morning he had made seventeen summary executions. Using the pistol that was seen as a daily ritual to Taxus. It was passed down from Emperor to Emperor. He finished, then went straight to work in finding the Reaper teams. Alex Cardis had gone missing now seventeen days and the new Imperium realized that the team had obviously turned on its masters and joined with Tiris. Then they had done the pre-emptive strike with the Dark Talon. But, before this, they had set up the Linsani station with a small amount of Bugs enough to show that they were in control of said species. Then whole merry hell had ensued with Dascoe setting them up. But he had gotten around to fitting a homing beacon on the *Defiant* as they had gone into the Dark Talon nest. He had been waiting for the *Defiant* in a small skiff that had been left untouched. He, then as the Reaper Teams had boarded, put a small radar pulse on the *Defiant*.

The Emperor Taxus walked slowly through to his new imperial office. Where he spent the next Thirty-two hours decoding and going over secret transmissions that the Imperium had intercepted. He knew that sub space frequencies were going hay wire but he had to try and home in on the *Defiant* he then after Twelve of those hours got hold of the radar pulse and tracked it down then he began to intercept the sub-space frequencies but only caught the last transmission between Cascoe and Tiris. One of his war council spoke up after hearing that they were about to meet up.

"Shall I engage a battlecruiser to finish them off?" Taxus pondered the question and thought, 'No I think not' "No" said Taxus, "they are going to be busy clearing up the mess on the Trill home world," He continued. "But keep tracking the *Defiant*. It's all running to plan," He said then carried on decoding the ghost chatter looking for deserters and mutineers, as usual he came across the odd one or two. And sent for them to be arrested immediately.

The fact that some of these so-called deserters were being set up by tech proficient Troopers who were fragging each other and several of them were innocent. This didn't occur to the new Emperor and even if it did, he executed anyway. He was running the Imperium with an Iron Gauntlet and things were going to schedule. He had nothing to lose. What he did have was a tendency to kill young boys.

They were invited to his quarters on a summons then he would slowly choke them to death. Nobody outside the Imperium war council knew about the sweet-meats. And the children's families were executed quietly, no connections. They were then tossed into a vat of acid. No bodies. But people going missing was a regular thing, it was all put down to rumours and superstition. Nobody broached the idea for fear of being next. The imperium was a shadowy cloak and dagger thing that was feared. And not to be underestimated. No hard times for the average civilian was bad enough but whole families going missing that was true fear. No one was safe, and no one was secure. It was a very secret and complex society with no scope to run and nowhere to hide.

No, under the new regime the Imperium's tyranny was absolute. They had the brief spell where they had freedom but that was never settled. No, when

Taxus took over they could feel the choke hold he had on the human race. Taxes, Terror forming and planetary rights were ceased he said as his declaration of his new found Imperial state, that the former Emperor had been lax and all this was about to change. He implemented new laws with tighter justice and hard-core sweeps of punishment. With execution being more and more in line with policies. He was announcing his word with authority, and no one was safe. And no matter what you did you knew that Fear and Terror was here to stay, most people signed up with the Navy and became Storm Troopers in the continuing battles known as the Faith Wars.

Tiris gripped wrists with Cascoe as the Tactical nuclear countdown carried on down to zero. Cascoe hated an action of this magnitude. This was worse-case scenario. And no one survived a Tactical nuclear strike. And that included the xenomorph that had swarmed over the Trill's home world. Tiris drank and smoked a stogie. Whilst he engaged in conversation with the Trill warlord.

They spoke for several hours about the new Emperor who had immediately shown his force of cast iron will. Whilst they engaged in conversation the strike carried on destroying every-thing. And reducing the once proud home world of the Trill to nothing but dust and ashes. The bug, well it was never getting off that planet. But it had done its purpose and done it to the utmost extreme. The bug had served its function. Now it was about to be decimated. Blown to absolute smithereens.

Now Cascoe had to meet up with the High King of the Trill and account for the trouble that had just about wiped out the Trill. How his intel should have been more on the ball. Anyway he couldn't be held accountable but knew he should have known that a biological weapon was on the cards, so to speak. But this xenomorph was fresh and had just been gathered up and used. If they had the proper intel they would have had counter measures. So now they had to figure out some weakness on the bug, no doubt that it was going to take a lot of studying on Bio mechanics and xenomorphic studies. It was a shame as the Linsani station that Tiris had blown up was a major key to the bug and it obviously was a staged fight between them on the *Defiant* and the Biological Tech heads who made the weapon. They needed to cover their tracks and get rid of the evidence of the Dark Talon. The risk that it was, was well played. They didn't mind playing the possum and knew if it was going to have to work they would have to sacrifice a number of Tech heads and a shitload of Troopers, Tiris noted this in his journal. And under-scored the words 'set up'. He didn't mention this to the rest of the Reaper teams. And with good reason. He knew if it was mentioned they would get on their high horse and everything would be at stake. He couldn't have this as they were in trouble enough with Taxus.

Knowing that the Lisani station was a set up was half the battle as he had a sneaky suspicion that they were carrying a small radar Pulse. He found its location on the rear of the *Defiant*. And Bucker went to the rear of the battlecruiser and found it and sent it flying away on a remote-controlled satellite. He smiled as he came back aboard.

"That's that done Sir".

Tiris locked on the satellite and sent it on its way. He turned a potential tragedy into a point of deception. A good player, that he was especially in covert deception and that set his mind at ease. He was always doubtful especially when the mission was as easy as that was. If something didn't add up question everything and I mean everything. Look at all the players in the scenario. Then look at the victims of the scenario and weigh up risks and possible out-comes, for both yourselves and the enemies, and if still something didn't add up then you question the questions until something turned those little alarm bells off. Tiris called this productive thinking. He was constantly in the productive thinking way of thought. And it always paid off. Years of training had led him to be an expert in the productive way of thought. Knowing that it was always a finely honed reason of thinking. He lit a new stogie and smiled as the tobacco curled and wisped from his breath in the area of the cockpit.

"Job well done," he said to himself then sat back and enjoyed his stogie. Then he opened up sub space wave alpha niner a private channel and spoke to Kurt.

"Hey Kurt."

Kurt flipped a couple of switches then replied. "Yes Tiris".

"Guess what a found on my ship earlier?" asked Tiris.

Kurt replied, "What?"

Tiris continued, "A dead man's pulse".

Kurt whistled through his teeth, "How did you manage to get a dead man's pulse on your ship?"

Tiris checked the channel made sure he wasn't being listened into. "Must have picked it up at the Linsani station".

Kurt laughed and replied, "Nothing that easy, goes that, simple always a catch".

"You got that right Kurt, you got that damn right. I thought that Kurt, I thought that".

They continued with their conversation for about ten minutes then signed off. They were on the right wave length. The Emperor, Taxus was mulling things over trying to find the right course for action. Especially since both Reaper squads were now mutinous and the Armour that was left was gone. And it would take a number of months to make new suits of the K11 power armour, seven months in total. But he had given the go ahead despite the length of time. He was hoping that these deserters would be brought to justice sooner. He was planning a trap one in which he would capture Tiris and the rest of them would be destroyed. He couldn't help wondering what chink in the armour Tiris had found, he had a rough idea and that was the pulse regulator and tracker were exposed, leaving the armour shorted out of power. Leaving the armour inert and useless. And thus, exposed to explosives. But now they had discovered it just made them protect the chest more. But Taxus knew that he had the advantage, training several Storm Troopers to use throwing blades and then the spider mine, explosives. This was the only way to do it. He immediately ordered the training of fifteen Storm Troopers with blades. Then they were backed up by five Troopers with spider mines. And this training was specific and thorough.

Chapter Twelve

They made the best plans they could to fight the Reaper teams, knowing that it was a pin point strike and they would have to be surgical in the strike. Precise and to the point of perfection, this meant lots of practice. They studied the trajectory of the weighted blades and began to implement their use in normal fights, giving them the-practice they needed. They practiced on the K78 armour which lacked the Reaper teams power but held a similar shape as the K11 armour, especially on the chest. The fifteen carried on the practice for weeks on end, just fighting and sleeping, sleeping and fighting they had no time to themselves and were bedraggled and worn out by the end of their training. But at the end they were competent enough to be used in the plans of the Emperor. He was forming an idea, an action, so to speak. He realised that the tracking pulse was jettisoned and was therefore useless to him. He smiled and said to himself 'Cleaver Reaper'. He then started to formulate a new plan, one with clever initiative and full-on destructive power. That's when he thought of the Pirates that were around Rygon Five, who were starting the distribution of Paradox narcotic into the surrounding systems.

Marcus was sat at the helm of his war destroyer when the alpha niner secure channel rang in his ears.

He sighed as he knew this day would only be a matter of time. "Yes your eminence?" He asked and switched all com links to silent making sure he wasn't disturbed.

"Taxus I understand the hastiness of this mission, but we wouldn't last five cycles against the Reaper Teams".

Taxus grinned and said, "Well you might if you have the full support of a garrison of my Storm Troopers".

Marcus sat back and replied, "A garrison, and what about the pay, how much?"

Taxus knew this question was on its way. "Fifty Billion per ship".

Marcus grinned he had seven war cruisers and knew that this was a healthy amount of Gold, credits. Enough for them to retire and live off profits from Paradox crystals. "It's a deal we will begin the hunt as soon as your garrison board our ships".

Taxus grinned, "Okay we will send said garrison soon as possible"

Chapter Thirteen

Tiris put the coordinates for them to go back to Orion. Where they would be safe for the mean time. They arrived at the station and as usual we greeted with howls and screams of enthusiasm. The station had been glad when the Reaper teams arrived they always were. Knowing they were still travelling around the universe was enough to keep hopes up. They were still taking in deserters and mutineers. But they knew that the Imperium had got wind of where they were. That's why they felt safer when the two squads of Reapers arrived. They had a new found respect for Tiris and the ship the *Defiant*. But they also had news on the sly, about the weakness that Tiris had discovered in the K11 power armour.

"It seems the Imperium have discovered the same flaw and are going to put it to full use in there campaign against you. It was one of the freshly absconded Troopers who had held a good rank before seeing his opportunity to desert.

Tiris shook his hand after speaking to him for at least half an hour about the tactics that they were going to use on the Reaper teams. Tiris stockpiled food and power packs for his laser carbines. He then went and dined with the owner of the station. Before he caught up with Bucker who had also been told about the chink in their armour. He wasn't worried as he knew that said flaw was hard to exploit and that the Storm Troopers were deserting more and more. This could only be a hindrance to the Imperium. They settled down to a night of wine and fine food. They felt the noose that was on their necks loosen. They settled down to a nice sleep cycle and did so for a few days and nights. They needed the rest and re-charge their batteries. Just as they were about to set off into the star system Kurt got in contact with an urgent message for Tiris.

"Tiris the Paradox Pirates are hunting you now and they have a full Garrison of Troopers on their ships."

Tiris smiled and said, "That figures Kurt".

Kurt was in a bit of a panic knowing his long time, amigo was in real trouble.

"Are they coming straight at us?" asked Tiris.

"Seems that way," he replied.

"Good," said Tiris, "I'm sick of this hiding shit, it's time to see if I can live up to the myth's"

Kurt asked the next question carefully trying not to sound like a coward. "Will you need me? or are you able to handle this?"

Tiris knew that Kurt was no coward but also knew that the man was useful if Tiris and the Reapers were finished. Then he would begin a mission to wipe out the Imperium. He would buy as many deserters and mutineers that he could, enough to put up a resistance against the severely Fascist Empire. Kurt had it in him to run the perfect missions against the Imperium he would also have the help from the Trill, who were half an army and space navy down after the Dark Talon ran its course on the Trill home-world. Tiris was in the mood for a showdown between him and the Imperium.

He set the coordinates to the centre of the star system. That was just outside the Orion system.

Tiris smiled, told Bucker to detach the *ESP* off of the *Defiant* and prepared for all Hell. He waited two sleep cycles then prepared for action. None of the crew or the Reapers got any sleep those two cycles. No they were in highly attuned emotions relying on their armour to stop them from sleeping. Then as if they had the clairvoyance, to know that the Pirates were closing in, the Pirates appeared.

The *Defiant* closed in on the first warship and began to light up the area with their plasma cannon. It melted through the hull of the first ship then the *ESP* fired its tactical missiles at the port and starboard sides of the warship. It did this and did it deftly, moving and winding around the hull and rear of the warcraft. Blowing apart the first ship. Then the second arrived just minutes before the warcraft number one went up in a flash and bang. The *Defiant* and the *ESP* were a good range away as the ship and all its crew went up. Bang. Whoosh, as the thing was reduced to molecules. And dust. The second warcraft didn't know what hit them as the concussion of the first ship hit them in a huge barrage of dead and dying matter.

Grimsford gulped, as the energy rushed right at his war cruiser. 'Damn' Thought Grimsford as the ship began to rattle and feel the energy of the first ship.

"Fuck they made light work of the first ship," he said, then the EMP hit the shit out of the second battlecruiser. The *Defiant* didn't waste a moment and shot straight at the laser cannons on the hull of the second cruiser and whilst they did this the *ESP* began to aim its plasma cannon at the crew quarters of the ship.

And tore through, decimating the men and metal. Then Bucker sealed their fate with his last two nukes, firing said missiles at the opened gash on the crews quarters.

Again the *Defiant* and the *ESP* raced to get out of the vicinity as the second ship was blown to smithereens. Tiris smiled and lit another fresh Stogie as the third came into the barrage of EMP and concussion of energy.

Tiris smiled and shouted out, "Fish Barrel".

The next manoeuvre was sheer magic The *ESP* settled its engines whilst the *Defiant* gripped onto the air lock and opened it and in marched the two squads of Reapers, First to go were the half a dozen or so of the Pirates who were not so sure what they were facing, a highly trained force of military power that couldn't be stopped.

The Troopers on board were switching on their night vision. As the warcraft was left without power. The pirates were left to suck on their Paradox masks whilst the Imperial Storm Troopers who had come to know this kind of action had an oxygen pump on each of their suits, But they still weren't a match for the Reapers, who were led by Dayton and Notsfur. The pair of them were expert demolition Troopers and knew the weakness of every ship they had boarded. This one in particular was its engine room at the rear of the ship.

The Reaper Dayton headed to the front of the ship, whilst Notsfur went to the engine room, each squad taking its time to finish both trooper and pirate as it got in the way. They then set the Thermite charges on both the rear and front, then left the ship. They went back on board the *Defiant* and drew away from the battlecruiser. And soon as it made a clear get-away they pushed the button. And a huge rush again as the ship was nuked from the inside out. The Reapers all smiled as the third ship was finished and its dust and particles again making the next ship inert. They then again began to circle the large warcraft. Who was still wondering what happened to the other three ships.

But it was too late as the *Defiant* again opened fire with its plasma cannon, this time aiming at their tactical nuclear missiles. This ripped the tail of the ship then bang and again the *Defiant* raced to get out of the way of its nuclear, meltdown and explosion. They got out and thought let's leave this place as The EMP was beginning to work on the *Defiant* who had a thing called cold shielding, a thing that was new to everyone, but Tiris had procured it when he found out the benefits of having cold shielding on its engine and vitals like oxygen and gravity. It cost a couple of billion for both the *Defiant* and the *ESP*.

"Best money I ever spent," he said then punched in the coordinates to get them away from there. They would head off back to Orion. They switched the thrusters on to maximum overdrive and got the hell out of there as they were running low on Missiles and the plasma cannon needed re-charging. They would do this by hiding out in the Orion's Mettalic grave yard and when the coast was clear they would head for a Tech twelve world and re-stock their missiles and recharge their plasma cannons. They had it all in hand and Tiris was growing more in combat every day. I mean he was already fearless being a full blown Colonel and the armour he wore was testament to the fact that no one could clip his wings.

He began the refuelling and re-stocking of Missiles and various other odds and ends like small space mines.

Nuclear ones they were a specialist Item and cost a small fortune, but worth it. He procured a good seventeen of them that were magnetic and exploded either by switch or self-detonated after a minute or so attached to the hull or outer shell. They had a blast radius of three kilometres and the EMP range was twice that. After they had restocked nuclear tactical missiles, enough to make three runs at whatever firepower they had, The *ESP* was the essential part in this campaign and Bucker knew it. He was a dab hand at the gorilla, tactics. Being as he was a top notch sniper specialist and had more kills than anyone else in the Imperium. He had a keen eye and a cold attitude, all his missions before he deserted were finished to more than satisfactory. He completed all missions and never once let the Imperium down. This was up until he met Tiris and jumped on board for the cause. It didn't take Tiris much explaining and showing Bucker the after effects of the Medusa seed. He was appalled at the Empires barbarism, He knew then at that instant after watching a full Trill warcraft turned to what only could be called slime. He was not a man to rattle easily and this was to him the only way to be, but after that show of toxic force he realised that he was gunning for the wrong side. So he made a pact with Tiris and they sealed it in a blood oath.

Bucker was satisfied with the conditions and knew that his part was to keep the other Reapers in check. This was done with the subtle art of being mindful. And knowing that if things went pear-shape he could settle down with the amount of credits that he had procured. Anyway, it was a small matter, He was the last person to complain. As he was one of the best soldiers that Tiris had ever known. This reflected in the two of their combat efficiency, they had good brains for tactics and never over exerted their command. This came as a great deal of trust by the pair of them knowing the two of them what to do and where to be in the scheme of things. That is why Bucker manned the small Scout ship *ESP*. He was a great pilot, smooth in his actions and deadly as an expert marksman could be.

Tiris was kind of like the opposite, he knew deployment and extraction techniques. He was a colonel and knew exactly what was going on with his squads, This recent campaign wasn't gained by luck, no sheer expert tactics by both himself and Bucker. And Tiris couldn't help but give himself a pat on the back for having the sergeant and knowing that the trooper was loyal and would follow him into the next life. It was complete and utter trust that the two of them had. Bucker docked with the *Defiant*. And turned off the engines of the *ESP*. Then he joined the rest of the crew, and they all settled into a sleep cycle.

Meanwhile the Pirates were mourning the loss of four of their warcraft. That left three and they knew that the Reaper squads were stronger and more cunning than they had first thought. They had a choice, wait and see if the Reapers would come back, or continue to track them down, it was one of those six and half a dozen questions that they had to answer and there were no absolutes in this.

Marcus was thinking and coming up with no answers. He knew the *Defiant* and the smaller but nimbler *ESP* were now re-arming and that would make them more deadly, more of a problem. He switched on the alpha niner channel and got straight in contact with the Emperor's right hand man. The gentleman took the news remarkably well and told him to sit tight as they had two Naval war cruisers in the vicinity and they would back him up.

Marcus sighed and replied, "They better be good, as Tiris made short work of four of my fleet".

The imperium's emissary smiled and said, "You were unprepared then, now you know".

Marcus scowled and thought, 'You're holding out on me'. He then carried on, he sent coordinates of his last three warcrafts whereabouts, so as to rendezvous with the Imperium's Storm Troopers. This would take a couple of days. And they knew the *Defiant* would come back and try to finish them off. Marcus hailed his other ships and told them the plan.

Both Grimsford and Coljax replied, "No problem Sir," said Coljax then Grimsford said the same. They headed to where the four warcraft had been destroyed. The area was totally rife with radioactive mess and played havoc with the remaining warcrafts instruments and support systems. But they stuck to the outer rim of the blast radius, and managed to stay low. The two war cruisers from the Imperium arrived after a short wait. Only half an hour later they had arrived. They sent a satellite probe into the centre of the radioactive mass that was all that was left from the battle that had happened. Battle no, the Reapers had made light work of the job, made the seasoned pirates seem infantile, useless, then they had disappeared into the Orion galaxy. And the Pirates who had arrived were left with no trace of the four war cruisers just static, all their comrades dead and the look on the first cruiser was that of child who didn't know his thumb from his dick.

The *Defiant* finished refuelling and re arming. And also restocking the troopers with tactical nuclear fusion grenades. And each of the troopers laughed as they got handed three each. They pinned them to their suits. What havoc had Tiris in mind. They knew it would be fun. And as was said earlier they were known to laugh all the way, all of them were hardcore knowing the score and leave them sore. But this was only part of the fun, when you watched the *Defiant* cause so much damage with the slinky stealth like *ESP* doing a great sneaky come out of nowhere attack. They revelled in the action. There was only one thing that made them happy and that was more action. They weren't trying to be heroes, no they were just doing as they were told. And that meant they were a credit to all the Storm Troopers in the known universe.

Chapter Fourteen

News of their war with the Pirates who were currently getting reinforcements with the two of the Empires best known battlecruisers. *Caldex* and *Reason*. They had been known to wreck many a Trill warcraft. But this was new to them. They were facing the elite Reaper forces. But they had the manpower and the firepower. Enough, with the help of the pirates they would divide and conquer. There orders were simple, render the *Defiant* inert, then board the vessel and arrest the two Reaper squads. But this was easier said than done. Apart from the armour being very near indestructible the men themselves were hand-picked special forces with medals up the Yin Yang.

Every one of them were highly trained and highly covert. No one, and I mean no one, had ever faced them and lived. They were originally meant to guard The Emperor. But Tiris had grown steadily sour towards the Emperor, he even had thoughts of killing the old Emperor. But this had worked out in his favour and the Trill had clinched it. The maniac knew he was for the firing squad. And shot himself with his own ceremonial pistol, one that he had used to execute deserters and mutinous rebels. The new Emperor was just as hands on if not more. He was executing them morning, noon and night. Taxus made sure the Storm Troopers stayed in line. And he knew this working because there were less and less to kill, he was balancing up the books so to speak, and the last Emperor wasn't as good as he should have been at uncovering the amount of disloyalty, that the Faith Wars had created. But Taxus had a good vice-like grip on the situation. And he wasn't about to release the grip until the Empire was back winning and now that Dark Talon had been used to full potential and had brought them from losing to all out wining. But the fact that the Reaper Teams both one and two were out their acting with no orders and without restraint. He felt as though he needed to make examples of them.

If he got hold of Tiris, he would behead him personally. But a fact is a fact and Tiris held the aces in his hand. Both teams of Reapers had deserted and that was serious as Tiris was a man not to be taking lightly. He had managed to out-manoeuvre and out-gun the Pirates. This had left the captain of the battlecruiser with a distinct cold feeling going down his spine. The ease in which the Reaper teams had decimated the four pirate war cruisers was sending warning messages to the Captain of the *Caldex*. He knew the Reaper teams and knew them well. It was going to be all out Hell when he locked horns with the *Defiant* and the *ESP*. But something was wrong, something just wasn't right. The captain excused it down to nerves. He was a seasoned veteran and stood by his principles. He had a no shit, can do way about himself you know nothing is impossible but some people are. He knew that he had to be ready for anything and I mean anything. The *Defiant* finished re-arming and re-stocking its troops with more ammo and more provisions.

Tiris smiled all the way, to and from the Tech twelve world. He was still chewing over what was round the corner. He knew one certainty that the Imperium would be next to come at him. He circled the area where he had decimated the Pirates staying just out of reach for the five battle cruisers and putting on his cloaking device so as not to seen by their radar. He smiled as the five ships slipped by and Tiris didn't say or do a thing. He then let go of ten of the space mines that he had bought, and laughed at the sheer genius of the plan. He then burnt an Ion force around the mines. So as to make the mines practically invisible. By the time they cottoned on to the mines it was too late. Two of the five battlecruisers had their hulls front and back blown to pieces. And the other three were rendered Inert by the EMP.

'Yes' thought Tiris as the five ships were in trouble. Two of which had no hope and the other three would have use as much power as they could to navigate the atomic mines, Nope, they were in a pickle. And they had no easy solutions but the *Caldex* and *Reason* were untouched but still in danger in the minefields. The *Caldex* began to shoot Ion lasers at said mines and this proved to be half the battle. Then the *Defiant* lived up to its name, turned right round and began its assault on the *Reason*.

Tiris told Bucker to, "stay piggy backed for now".

Bucker was itching to get right in there about the action but knew that Tiris didn't call the shots for nothing. He was the Reapers leader and that was enough for Bucker, he called the shots and was never wrong. He was a calculating head of the squads, the main man. All the Reapers thought highly of him and what do you know, he never let them down. He proved to be in control and no wonder he was the squads. He hadn't lost a reaper yet. And planned not to do so, and that was all the squads needed to know. He made sure their shit was wired tight and if, and it was a big if, something went wrong they know he could handle it.

The *Defiant* aimed its plasma cannon at the ships main deck. Where the *Reasons* Captain was standing at the helm. Watching as the *Defiant* opened fire straight at the man. The cannon shot its energy particle beam and straight away tore a huge hole in the deck where the Captain stood, he took the brunt of the weapon. Then, the *Defiant* shot forth two mines into the big gaping wound on the front of the ship. Soon as they attached themselves to the metal gash on the front of the *Reason* then they pushed the detonate button and blew the thing to smithereens, they had no chance. It was a surprising manoeuvre and wasn't in line with what the captain of the *Reason* thought or expected to happen. I mean he thought, 'deserters on the run, constantly running, would be to use hit and run tactics, no it caught him way off guard. But then nothing the Reaper teams did was by the book. They were operating without regulations, there was no Parlai, no stand up and settle this properly no, the Reaper squads knew on thing and that was no mercy. Anyway, the *Caldex* opened fire soon as it got a clear vantage point on the *Defiant*. But the *Defiant* had a trick or two up its sleeve. And Bucker climbed on board of the *ESP* and smiled laughed and said, "Ready when you are Boss".

Tiris counted down from five and the *ESP* separated from the *Defiant*. Bucker then switched on his cloaking device and hid in the scrap and ruins of the *Reason*.

He waited as he was twice as lethal when undercover. He aimed a tactical missile at the last remaining Pirate ship. He saw his chance and sent the missile thrusting straight at the battlecruiser. Its target was the same as before, the missiles that were housed on its left-hand side. It also had tactical missiles housed on the other side. But Bucker decided not to over exert his reach. And started to head towards the *Caldex*. Again putting up its cloaking device the *ESP* was a strength of smoke and laser. He then fired the first chance he got, at the *Caldex*. Ripping the *Caldex* in half with the high energy laser. Its Troopers sent up a surrendering message. They now knew that few and far between, they were no match for the Reapers. They flew the white banner of surrender. They were then let on board and the captain of the vessel was taken away to be interrogated. By Bucker and Tiris.

They scuttled what was left of the *Caldex* then got right down to brass tacks. He didn't say a word as Tiris grilled the Capitan hard and brutally, he was giving the choice a cyanide capsule or join the gallant Heroes of the *Defiant* he chose the capsule. And died a strangulating death with his hands clawing at his throat as the deadly substance started to work. Tiris stood over ham as he gasped for air. He shook his head and the Captain watched as Tiris did so.

"A waste of a good Trooper," said Tiris as the man croaked it.

Bucker saddened by the act of self-sacrifice stood fast and said, "Do we give him an honourable burial?"

Tiris sniffed and said, "shit yeah, Any man who is willing to sacrifice himself deserves an honourable burial and on a personal note I would do myself with my Pistol rather than ingest poison".

Bucker sighed and said, "Me too boss."

The rest of the Troopers were taken to a tech five world and left to get on with it, after their radios and communication links were severed, of course. Kurt Lidel smiled when he heard the news on the *Defiant*. "I take it you are as good as the myths say."

Then he punched in the coordinates to Rygon Five. He then opened up the Alpha niner channel, "Slip cord, this is your Angel".

He waited, knowing that it may be in the midst of nuclear break down. That meant he may be flying blind and deaf, "Slip Cord this is your Guardian Angel. Come in?" He adjusted the frequency and carried on hailing the *Defiant*. Then after a short while he got a response from the *Defiant*, "Slip cord here over".

Kurt smiled, "Okay Tiris where are the Troopers that surrendered?"

Tiris smiled, "they are safe for the mean time. What should I do, I left them without radio comms on a tech five world".

Kurt laughed, "Classic". He said as he drew his ship closer to Rygon Five. "You wanna meet up and chew the shit?"

Tiris smiled and lit another stogie, "When?" He asked.

Kurt punched the orbital scanner to make sure the Imperium hadn't left anything behind. "When can you get to the Rygon system?"

Tiris puffed on his stogie, "I'll be there day after tomorrow".

Kurt signed himself out and said, "Tech five huh," and began to laugh. A deep throaty laugh.

Tiris looked out into the deep vacuum that was space. And punched in the coordinates to meet up with Kurt and chew this latest conquest up and tell it exactly as he had called it. Then he would part company with Kurt and try and find some work. He wasn't too thrilled at having to sell more Paradox. But then hey why the Hell not.

Chapter Fifteen

He arrived at Rygon Five and noticed the ship of Kurt's in orbit waiting for the *Defiant* then two sleep cycles later he had imparted all the gory details of the space battle. He was even laughing as he continued to dominate the better part of sixteen hours, drinking energy boosting drinks and smoking cigars. This was the pinnacle of Kurt's journey as he had a powerful bond with the Reaper squad's colonel. And it showed in his boozy, alert eyes. He wouldn't betray him, not for all the Gold credits in the known universe. No this Colonel was in a class of his own and no one could dispute that. He made light work of the enemy and came up trumps with the spirit of comradery. He was a fucking lucky charm and Kurt knew this. That was why he tracked him and it was known by Tiris that the man was tracking him. But he had saved his life more than five times and that was why he was Guardian Angel.

Tiris smiled as they parted company. Kurt and him were tight and I mean tight, Kurt was the only one that Tiris trusted outside his squads, I mean, well he had Cascoe but there were years of distrust between Tiris and Cascoe but he had managed to smooth things over. Between the Warlord and himself, this hadn't been easy to begin with, but Tiris showed willing and complete and utter faith between the two of them. That was his next port of call, The Trill war hero, but this was easier said than done as after wiping out the Dark Talon he had vowed never to be that vulnerable again and he intended to keep his word on that. He set a gauntlet of war cruisers on the remaining five planets that inhabited the Trill. This wasn't just a show of force, no. they could handle anything that the Imperium sent their way. And they knew that they would be tested in the most desperate of battles.

The Dark Talon was only one of the Imperium's many weapons of war. And they knew they would have a difficult time in front of them. The Imperium were designing a new Power Armour. The same specs but the armour was twice as powerful as the Reaper armour with no flaws. It was called Titan reaper and was just fourteen days away from completion. It was an actual exo-skeleton that kept the Troopers safe. The Helmet was the same except larger. It had the best AI in the Universe, they never missed. And as for the power and grav field it had a cold shielding that covered the armours power battery. This made them invulnerable especially against nuclear and fusion weapons.

They were even protected from Plasma cannons. The one weapon that the Reaper squads were twitchy about. This was scepticism at its best as none of the Reapers had gone up against a plasma wielding Trooper. But early tests rendered the weapon as useless. This was worked into the new Titan Reapers armour. This was as good as it got, now they had to pick their squads. They were looking at ex-military Prisoners. Murderers with no ethics and nothing to lose. They were considered as too deadly to be counted amongst the normal Storm troopers. No these were hardcore and whole lot more of killers, and thieves. They were most of them picked right before execution and shown into the Military R and D were they were mesmerised by the toys and machines that were under research.

Then the new owners of the new armour were trained in secret to the abilities of the Titan Reaper suites. They were kept in a specialist space station way on the rim of the Spinward Marches. Where they would acclimatize to the suit's enhancements and they got a real feel of power. This sent the already insane troopers really insane. There were two squads of seven, And they needed no more. The Titan reaper armour K one, one eight was totally enhanced and had no flaws it was totally invulnerable. But they had said the same about the K Eleven armour and all its glory and it was true, but technology changed so quickly and more and more the Imperium advanced in ways that would turn your hair white. With biochemical warfare being as one of the things it was working on. You know things like the Medusa Seed, also the Dark Talon. Oh they were racing forward in fields of toxins that drive you insane and monsters that even the stoutest of hearts would shudder at. No the Imperium was far from finished, in the Faith Wars they were using more and more new weapons every day and that was why Tiris had committed, Treason.

He saw their test on mutants and that had appalled him to his very core. They were splicing and enhancing Troopers with the nasty bugs that were being made in the laboratories. The Troopers signed on for the experiments and they were usually dead within a week or so. But he had also seen it turn on its captors and render it asunder and destroy the science division and all its military support. This he had witnessed first-hand as he was asked an assortment of questions by the old Emperor. He responded in general, that his opinion was not as valued as he thought and then responded, "Accidents Happen your Eminence" He said.

Knowing that he was supposed to give an in-depth account of what had happened. But it was gruesome and he didn't have the skills to know exactly what had just happened. So he just bit his tongue and remained impassive. Knowing any acts of the man's defiance would be picked up and he would be executed post-haste. He breathed a little easier as the Emperor waved him away accordingly. Sixteen sleep cycles later and him and the other Eight Reapers were gone, they had executed the perfect mutiny. Stole a reliable Scout ship and jumped world. To go and commit Treason. By stealing the stats on the Medusa seed. And sell them to the emperor's worst enemy. The Trill. The Faith Wars were on going all over the place. They stuck to the outer rims of the Marches until they had the time to meet with Cascoe and this had all happened before they met with their utmost enemies the Titan Reapers. Tiris buckled up and sent the *Defiant* straight towards the other home world of the Trill. The one that the high King liked the least. It was the last place the Emperor Taxus would think of destroying, He had given it the utmost of thought into why he would go there and it occurred to him that the last place they would look was first place they mistook. He was surrounded by his most honoured guard the High Trill. They had been alerted straight away about the Dark Talon. As apparently they had specifications on said bug. And immediately evacuated the High King and his family. Now they had to strike back somehow and being as it was nearly half of the Trill's armies and most of its civilian population. But hoped still burned in the hearts of the Trill and knowing that the Medusa Seed was inert and of no use they had started the bugs up and sent them into battle they had no orders only the feeding and killing frenzy that filled the monsters with spirit. They knew nothing else and sixty thousand of these things swarmed over the Trill home-world. And nearly sent The Trill into genocide. This was exactly why Tiris had stopped being loyal to the Imperium.

He opened comm links to Cascoe, "Cat man do its rip cord come back?"

He waited a minute or so then signalled again, "Cat man do this is rip cord over?"

Cascoe smiled as he signed a legion of soldiers into his command. "Rip cord this is cat man do will open Alpha niner channel copy".

So he punched the intercoms secure link.

"How the hell are you Cascoe.?" Came Tiris Cords voice.

Cascoe smiled and said, "I'm doing away, could be better".

"You get the result you deserve Tiris".

Tiris half snorted a laugh and replied. "Boy did I. You hear about the new Reaper armour?" Cascoe chuckled "Yes I did it's just the best they got now. Already they've done four sweeps on the front lines at Sigmus".

Tiris knew something was off, as he hadn't heard of that particular campaign.

Cascoe let him go silent for a couple of seconds then carried on. "They are combat effective but not too bright or well trained. But dangerous, highly dangerous, taking hits from all sides and not even breaking sweat."

Tiris blew out another match, "I take it we are needing to plan a strategy?"

The question settled in Cascoe's mind. "We will meet you on the rim of Sigmus and we will give you all the details on the Titan Reaper squads".

Tiris nodded and replied, "Yes Cat man do, we will be there".

Cascoe smiled and said, "We'll meet at Sigmus twelve the Starport, on the outer rim of Sigmus".

Tiris replied, "That'll do just fine we need to see each other and plan our next victory".

Cascoe laughed out loud at this, his voice thinning into a hiss.

"Rip cord out," came the last statement from Tiris.

They then both headed towards the Sigmus quadrant on the edge of the Marches. Taxus knew he was winning when he heard the Titan Reapers had done four sweeps and come up with maximum fatalities. And no casualties. They were totally prepared for anything that would try and take them down. They were psychotic enough to greet anything and I mean anything, not that their first four campaigns had turned out exceptionally well for them and they came out of the campaigns without a scratch.

Immediately they were pinned with medals for valour and courage. They were above and beyond in the capabilities and knew it. They could withstand anything. Taxus was patched instantly through to the Titans.

"Gentlemen you have ushered in a new era with Cybernetics. And as predicted you have shown great skill and great Martial Tactics".

The Captain of the Titans, Contrill, who was a serious psycho path who had murdered ten Troopers over a game of Poker, smiled and said, "Piece of cake".

Taxus noted him, and put a serious amount of credits in his account, "That was just perfect," He said. He should have used the military prison for the first two squads. But no point in crying over spilled milk. He carried on as they were each pinned with a medal of valour knowing that any of a culmination of things could have happened. But "yes" he said as he watched the second sweep. The way they took care of the Trill was bordering on magic. That and the way they used their AI helmets was well, out of sight. He spoke briefly to the two squads saying how this project and the Dark Talon project had superseded his expectations and he would use both projects again in the hunting down and killing of the Trill High King and all his consorts.

Contrill was growing fond of the new found emperor but had little to judge the new found Eminence. I mean six months ago he was due to be executed now he was practically his right hand man. No, he had to count his blessings on this and he thought the man a crook who had landed lucky in his serving posts. This had led to Contrill being first in the line to be put forward for the Titan project. It was two squads of seven. And the leader of the second company was a Major Narsill who was supposed to have links to Tiris. But nobody broached the subject with him as he was quick to temper and hard to calm down. He never showed any signs for being anything other than a cheating murdering thief. He had come up the same time as Tiris and this was taken into account. But whether the two of them had been cohorts well this was why he lost his temper whenever the subject came up. No he wasn't even on the same page as the colonel. In fact the whole made up story that they were cadets together had been fabricated. That's what angered him so much. But the Major knew that there was some sort of gain from the story and what it was only the Emperor knew. He supposed it was meant to keep the ranks from falling into disrepute. But edge or no edge, it riled him up. And if you carried the rumour too far you would find yourself on the edge of his bayonet and you'd have to be some kind off suicidal freak to even mention the relationship with the two of them. Especially since he got released into the Titan project. He was however harbouring a grudge against the Colonel and only he knew why.

The Major Narsill was a standalone, every man for himself guy. Tiris and Cascoe gripped each other wrists, and patted each other on the back. "Hey Cat man do how you are holding up?"

The question, that was simple to answer was hard to endorse. As Cascoe kept his feelings on the matter under strict silence. He rolled his eyes and smiled at the colonel then replied, "I'm fine, I mean most of my crew and many of the other crews are finding it tough to deal with but you know the old saying, all is fair in love and war".

Tiris sniffed and said "Yes I suppose it is. It does not excuse the low lying every dirty trick in the book using a megalomaniac that just took over son of a bitch".

Cascoe released his grip and looked the colonel dead. "This aint over Colonel".

Tiris put his helmet on his waist. And the two warlords headed to Cascoes quarters and indulged themselves in wine and food. They made it a night to remember as the two of them knew they wouldn't be getting together for a long, long time and it was nice to impart the blessings of a nice meal and good company. 'Yes' thought Tiris, after this was all over they would have to make this a regular thing. That's if the two of them lived, knowing that the two of them had one hell of a fight in front of them. It was marked in their destiny and there was no way around it. They enjoyed each-others company and served themselves well. The rest of the Reapers were down the galley mixing with the Trill who were fully aware of the service that the reapers had done for them. And knew that they were under no threat from the Reaper Squads and the reaper squads knew the same. A good time was had by all.

Tiris and Cascoe spoke about the new Emperor and his immediate actions to weed out deserters. Then he would execute the main perpetrators in a very public way showing no mercy and keeping the rest of them in line. But more and more Troopers were deserting the Storm Troopers. And this was damn right, thought Tiris. The more he tightened his grip the more they hated his oppressive nature. It was a sign of the times, and Tiris was only one of many Troopers that had deserted the Imperium. And as far as he was concerned that was damn right. They dined and drank most of the night then Tiris headed back to his ship feeling a little drunk, he bedded down and fell into a pleasant slumber. After the eight hour sleep cycle Tiris woke with a mild hangover, nothing he couldn't handle. He took some pills that sorted it straight away. He called on the rest of his Troopers to get back onto the *Defiant*, they did so without any complaints. Tiris then did a system check and punched in the coordinates to take them to Rygon

Five. He smiled with the Stogie in his mouth, "Right lads," he said, "We got problems".

Then he played the recording he had gotten from Cascoe. "This is the new and improved Reaper suits". Then they all watched as they tore through a good hundred Trill lightning blue soldiers. The Trills hardest hitting soldiers, and this led to the Reapers having serious doubts on whether they would survive an encounter with the Titans. They watched in shock as the Titans, took hit after hit, lasers and high energy plasma cannons. But nothing even shook them, that was a fact a cold motherfucking fact. But Tiris remained upbeat and carried on with his excursion to Rygon Five. They arrived a few short hours later, and began to negotiate the sale of as much Paradox as they could get into the hold. Bucker on the other hand was re-arming the *ESP*. He needed to get as many tactical missiles as he could. And also re-stock the sand throwers at the rear of the *ESP*. He smiled as he did this.

He knew of two certainties, one he was about to be involved in the fight of his life and two he might not live through it. 'To Hell with it you got to die of something,' he thought and he carried on with the racks of missiles, nuclear ones as well. He smiled as the last of the sand was loaded onto the rear of the *ESP*. And he docked onto the *Defiant* and they headed away into the Stars as they were going to the Outer Rim of the Marches, back to Orgis two. There they would line up buyers for the Paradox Crystal, enough to double the profit of what they had spent. Which was about twelve million Credits. This would be doubled and put straight into the kittie. They had no need for anymore profit but were going to sell the Paradox for, well, for something to do. They had no need for anything that was too extravagant. No, the Missiles and the Paradox was just the thing that they needed.

They put on the cloaking device as they headed to Orgis two. It was kind of hairy round that way with the Faith Wars spilling out of the Marches. And into the Orgis system, they would orbit around the systems major populated planet Sixmus, that was practically in the middle of the Orgis system with three suns keeping the planets in the nearby vicinity alive and flourishing. Sixmus in particular. Sixmus had a reputation for being a meeting point for deserters and mutineers. Taxus had no idea about the Orgis system. Well he had a little bit of an idea that the Orgis system was housing a lot of mutineers but every time he investigated it came up blank. As if someone had tipped them off. He was sure someone was helping the Troopers desert, and he was growing more and more impatient. And further and further from the truth. He was already considering executing his current council. And replacing it with fresh blood. But this would have to wait as he was sure his next move would be a cunning and sly one. He would make preparations to catch Tiris, the trap was a simple one, an old decrepit Trill warcraft sending out an SOS. The battlecruiser was a type two war craft and it did hold four hundred Trill soldiers. But they had died. Apparently bloodily so it, was a massacre and it was the Titan Class reaper that had done the damage. They were sending the distress signal every four minutes. Claiming that they were down to skeleton crew and were low on fuel. Most of the weapon systems had been destroyed and what was left was inert.

The *Defiant* came upon the distress signal and Tiris knew exactly what to do, he switched the comms to Alpha niner. "Guardian Angel this is rip cord do you copy?"

Kurt caught the transmission and replied, "Yes rip cord this is Guardian Angel, what's up?" "I have a strange beacon giving off a SOS every four minutes".

Kurt set his diagnostic to scan the local sector and try and figure out what was going on with the vessel. He picked up the beacon and went straight on the comm link to the war craft.

"Sir, we have received your distress call and are on route to save you, just hold tight."

Then Tiris got a small sense of foreboding, Something wasn't right, he could feel the ship was a tomb, but no that wasn't it, it was something else. And only way of knowing for sure was to board the vessel. He set the ship to Automatic and headed in the direction of the distress signal. He shot through the system heading for the distress call. He switched the comm link to alpha Niner and haloed Guardian Angel.

"Guardian Angel This is rip cord do not enter that ship, I say again do not engage with that ship."

Guardian Angel received and believed. "That's a negative on docking with the ship. Is that right Rip cord?"

Tiris settled himself down. "Angel This is Rip cord yes, that's a niner on boarding that ship until we arrive." Kurt smiled and said, "That man has a nose like a bloodhound".

He then settled the engine on his scout craft and sat there dormant, waiting for the reaper teams to arrive. And when they did arrive he was expecting fire power and a tonne of it. He waited one maybe two sleep cycles when just as he was about to burn those orders he just got, the *Defiant* arrived.

"Thanks Angel I'll handle it from here Rip cord out."

Then the *Defiant* began docking procedure at the rear of the Trill battlecruiser. The *ESP* settled into a central sweeping pass to make sure everything was kosher, Bucker centred a laser on the middle of the craft and two tactical missiles aimed at the weapons housing on the second deck. They had tactical inter stellar nuclear missiles, half the ship long, one on each side of the elongated starship. These were just in case things went all to shit and there was no way of saving the planet, as they had done on the Trill home-world. But Tiris decided to keep it civil and reaper team two boarded first. Then Reaper team one boarded after waiting three or four minutes watching the Reaper team two's back. They got passed the galley were food and supplies were kept. Then they passed med bay one. He was really right this time no this was no tomb no it was a giant bomb.

Tiris screamed the order to retreat, "Both Squads back now!" The two reaper teams did so and did so fast, They made it back just as the ship went into full nuclear meltdown, Tiris punched in the coordinates and Bucker and Kurt shot off first. Knowing that they would be spearheading the *Defiant* away from the interstellar nuclear explosion They made it by the skin of their teeth. And settled down as the debris and dusted went by them. That was a good sign. They had just enough time to get out of there. Tiris removed his skull and got in contact again with Guardian Angel.

"Angel this is rip cord over. Angel this is rip cord over," He waited just under a minute until he got a response.

"Rip cord this is Angel do you copy?"

Tiris smiled and replied, "Yes Angel thought we had lost you there".

Kurt smiled through his Skull helmet, "It was just a matter of time if you hadn't appeared when you did, I was going to board that booby trap."

Tiris was laughing as his Guardian Angel said this, "Well Kurt I wasn't sure until the ship got scanned by Bucker then I noticed the two Intergalactic missiles were warm. That meant someone had lit them up and waited. Then they put them in stasis until the docking procedure was put on, then they had a short fuse and boom. But like I said the missiles were put on stasis and that gave me the skin crawling sensation I usually get when something aint right".

Kurt sighed and said, "Thank fuck for hunches".

Tiris punched in the ship to settle into an idle manoeuvre. Whilst he set the controls to standby he opened the other Channel alpha niner.

"Bucker can you report quickly,?"

Bucker haloed him back, "Yes sir be right there".

Chapter Sixteen

Taxus got the news that the trap had failed and that the *Defiant* had escaped. "That fucker Tiris has more lives than a trill domesticated cat". He signed the execution orders on seventeen Troopers that morning. And four of them were sergeants and use to be extremely loyal to the Imperium. He had been Emperor for less than two months and he was already passed the most blood thirsty of them, he had racked up two hundred executions and a large percentage of these were by his own doing, he didn't mind getting bloody in fact he kind of enjoyed the acts. He got through to his main public official a Paradox using man who was known for having a very aggressive nature, especially when under pressure. The man's name Cerbrius. He was head dog of war. He had personally over seen the new armour, 'Titan Reaper.'

"Yes your Eminence?," came the question from Cerbrius.

Taxus smiled as he washed his bloody hands in the Marble sink. "How the fuck did he escape from that trap?"

Cerbrius punctured his nerve ending with Paradox and replied after a sure fire rush going to his central nervous system. "I have no idea how your Eminence. It must be blind luck".

Taxus growled and said, "Step up the searches, he must have ties to the deserters. Double the bounty on Tiris' head, as well".

Cerbrius smiled as the rushes that were more trippy than smack like, coursed through his nervous system. He, after a short second silence replied, "Yes your Eminence"

Taxus thought, 'There is nothing like a loyal and blood thirsty dog'.

Taxus growled and let the thought of him being swarmed by deserters leave his mind and settle his nerves, he snarled and went into the co habitation room where there were six or seven young women lying around, three of them he had choked unconscious then the rest he had beaten to death, with the bit of a bolt action armour piercing sniper rifle, a relic one of the many antiques of death that he kept, sometimes he used said instruments in enacting his sordid sexual and all too often violent acts. He had a lot of anger in him and the station he held was in prime position for him to act out his aggressive cold and bloody fantasises and nobody could say a word (nobody dared), no they had too much to lose. And people can and did vanish under his totalitarian leadership.

Tiris headed back out to Rygon Five. The *Defiant* was loaded with enough armament to destroy a small moon. I mean to atoms. He orbited the planet that was a Titan tech twelve world. That was the main planet in the Marches that manufactured Paradox. There were others but Rygon Five was the most prevalent with the product travelling to all out posts on all systems. It was a major problem that everybody knew about but let it be as no one was sure who was running the Crystal, some say the Imperium, others said it was the Trills way of laughing at the Imperium, but more than likely it was both. Some even said that it was the reason the Faith Wars were on going,

Tiris left that thinking to the scholars and historians. But couldn't help but see to his own materialistic side. No, he wasn't greedy and he made sure his Troopers were taken care of. He hadn't a problem with a little profit. Some would say he was a true mercenary, a soldier of fortune, He smiled and puffed on his stogie. Tiris replayed the conversation with the Linsani world's space station about the Dark Talon, He thought why they would hire him and how did they manage to track him down, It was a guess but an educated one. He thought the dead man's pulse must have been put on before they got to the Lisani station with the dark talon. He was thinking that the mercenary Dascoe had obviously put the pulse on the *Defiant* but had done so before he returned to the Linsani Station and woke the Talon up, then lit up the pulse as he retreated away.

Bucker taught him similar methods in his guerrilla tactics and sabotage techniques. He was, as far as Bucker saw, too good and had aced the snipers academy and had left without a single regret. In fact Dascoe had gone against the grain and challenged Bucker to a contest in all aspects, Bucker had left the pupil of his barely breathing but alive. Then he had been the most decorated soldier in the Troopers With twelve warlord's killed by him from smoke and mirrors situations. Then he had met with Tiris who offered him a place in his squad. Bucker had been wary at first but Tiris diminished his fears and proved to him that his squad were the best solution and that solution was to desert.

After some time of thinking about it Bucker knew it was his best option. Especially after watching the Medusa Seed work and sensing the Imperium was only in it to either enslave the Trill or wipe them out all-together. They were winning up until Tiris leaked the Medusa Seeds chemical formula. Bucker had his hands on the situation all along. And was true to his new Colonel, knowing deep inside if he wanted to, he could destroy the two reaper teams. But he left those thoughts by the wayside, as he knew that Tiris wasn't in it for the credits, he wasn't in it for the glory. He was in it to speed up the end of the Faith Wars.

This was a very trying situation for Tiris as he knew that Bucker was the only link in the chain that could be exploited. But Bucker was quiet and complacent. Didn't show any reason to be against Tiris. But Tiris knew and Bucker knew that he knew. They headed to Rygon Five, Bucker was piloting *ESP* with remarkable ease, an attribute that he had honed through many years in service to the Imperium. He was indeed a skilled pilot and had shown his wings with a degree of skill and cunning. His ability was only matched by two, maybe three, pilots in the Marches, Tiris was one of them. Another reason for Bucker to admire the Reaper leader. They got to Rygon without any encounters, the fact was, it was too quiet and Tiris didn't like that, he could sense a foreboding, something was amiss, He didn't know what but he knew it was close. As they orbited the Planet Rygon they were reminded of how much the Paradox Crystal was worth. They made another purchase, this time to take to the rim of Imperium controlled space, it was a bit risky but Tiris knew the only way to make more credits was to take chances.

They all took off their power armour and dressed in civilian scout attire. They would need to blend in, Bucker put the *ESP* into docking mode with the *Defiant*. He walked into the ships hold and then took off his power armour. All their suits were closed into a locking system that even the best thieves would not be able to gain access to. No, not without the mother codes and retinal scan from TIris. They boarded a light space station used by off world personal to trade and barter for their economic gain. They were instantly greeted by the police state that was the Imperium Cyborgs and muscular policemen kept a watchful vigil on the comings and goings in the Station and surrounding planets. They were looking for escaped convicts who had managed to escape the death penalty, seventeen of them to be precise, but they had caught four and that had left thirteen still at large. They amount of gold credits on their heads was obscene.

Tiris punched into his wrist locater the facial and DNA of the thirteen men. He had a rough idea where they were headed and that was a way aways at the Orion system, where most deserters ended up sooner or later, he brokered the deal for the tonne of Paradox and made him and the rest of the Reapers another three billion Credits. They gathered some food and drink and some odds and ends, you know Stoggies and wine. The Colonel was doing a little research that was very sketchy at best, he was trying to find out what squadron the deserters had deserted from. The question was usually answered with, "I know nothing".

They then patched into the Imperiums most wanted list, and yes he was top of that list him and his Reaper Team in ascending order. But he figured out how they had escaped a prison transport and managed to fly off on a small Scout ship that was piggy backing the large transport. The leader of the thirteen, a sergeant in the death squad that had been at the front of the attacks in the Faith Wars and were among the most commandeered of Troopers had seen to it his platoon captain was killed at night and then posted his head to the Imperium's Generals.

They had only just managed to capture the leader called Ike Tooms. When he had seen his opportunity to escape from the prison ship that was taking them to be executed by Taxus himself. He had seen the ion trail out of the side window and noticed that it was fully fuelled and he knew the timing of the Troopers on the Guard shift. They passed by as Tooms lay groaning and cold sweating something that he had trained in at the Imperium. The Trooper smiled thinking 'This one aint going to make it to Terra'. He checked in then opened the Iron Door. Tooms lay there groaning and sweating as the Trooper pointed his rifle at the incapacitated and shivering trooper.

"Okay Tooms whenever you are ready to pass into the next realm."

Tooms relaxed and began to Hiss and spit as if taking a severe seizure. The Trooper who was green as he was a vegetable, made the classic mistake and went to kick the lying dormant Sergeant. Tooms span and swept the feet out of the Guard. Then he took full initiative and scooped up the man's weapon and let off a burst off splitters. That ripped the guards armour and body killing him. He grabbed the guards pass key and let out the seventeen prisoners all of whom were on death row. Tooms got all except four of them to the scout craft that was piggy backing on the Prison Ship. Now to escape the clutches of the tyrannical madman that was the Emperor Taxus.

They headed for safe haven in the Orion system. They sped away whilst the prison transport took inventory of what the deserters had stolen and how many guards they had killed, that number was seventeen and loss of four to them so about equal. Tooms was also a star rated Pilot and the best in his regiment. He was nowhere as good as Bucker but still made a tricky enemy. And he hollered and whooped as they shot off onto space. They were armed but didn't have any armour so the first thing they would do was get some credits. They would do this by robbing a tech ten outpost of about Seven billion gold credits. This gave them the option of buying some K seventy eight armour at around seven million a suit. This also gave them the option of being incognito and blend in with the Troopers around the local systems to Terra. They would use this advantage to the utmost efficiency. They had a series of robberies and general piracy. Pillaging and an assortment of crimes against the Imperium. They were needy, greedy and full of thievery.

Tiris admired Tooms and his squad of miscreants. They were his kind of soldier they had shown the kind of grit that only he experienced as being a deserter himself. But he absolutely had to make the point of meeting Tooms and his renegades. He sent a message to the Starport in the Orion nebula, being as it is a haven for the crooked and lost. He sent it to the direct attention of the owner and chief of the Starport in the Graveyard. Of destroyed ships and hulks of mass rusting wreckages. He left the message to be seen only by Toom's deserter and soldier of the Faith Wars. The Message comprised of a series of codes that would put him straight through to Tiris and only Tiris would be able to decipher.

It was the only way he would get a straight answer was codes and more codes. And he was totally needing to make the point of shaking Tooms hand. For such a defying and chaotic move. No Tiris had a boasting point and loved to meet fellow deserters and swap stories and chew the shit. But Tooms had escaped twice and made a reputation for himself. And this is why Tiris was on the mission to meet Tooms. Below all the Reaper squad on the most wanted list was Tooms and his fellow Pirates. But the Imperium was kicking into full swing, and that was with the Titan Reapers, who were just preparing themselves for their onslaught on Tiris.

Bucker was still in charge of the *ESP* and was proud of the fact. Tiris waited on the outer rim for a reply. It was seven sleep cycles later when the coded message came through. Tooms smiled as he patched himself through on the secure channel. "Hey Tooms, you copy?"

Tooms responded, "Hey Chord. How the hell are you?"

Tiris puffed a little on his stogie, "I'm fine Tooms, loving your handy work".

Tooms laughed a small jesters laugh, "Yep pretty sick and slick".

Tiris looked at the end of his stogie, "Yeah we gonna meet sometime?"

Tooms laughed some more, "Yeah we should, you are about the only one that I can truly trust".

Tiris Puffed some more "Yeah, how far are you away?"

Tooms smiled and said, "About two sleep cycles away."

Tiris let out a little laugh, "Yeah we can wait".

"See you in two". Tooms carried on smiling.

"See you in two". He replied.

Then Tiris switched off the secure channel and told the rest of the reapers that Tooms was on his way. They sat in stasis waiting for Tooms and his thirteen deserters. They would meet up for a good session of drink and food. Where they size each other up and swap stories of space mutinies and sticking the middle finger up at the Imperium. And they knew each other so they were planning on filling the tankard and living it up. Probably for several days. This was the general idea. And Tiris was hoping to make a new friend. This wasn't all he needed, he also needed to see if there was any information about the Titan Reapers. As sooner or later they were going to cross paths with them. The second sleep cycle finished and Tooms and his miscreants boarded The *Defiant*.

First thing they noticed was the men were all casually dressed as they were powering up their armour readying for whatever the Imperium was about to throw at them. And the Linsani were making progress in the Dark Talon biological weapons. They were trying to get them out of their Hiving habits and act more with free will. And manage to fight more ferocious and with more clean kills. This was proving tricky as their hunger and blood lust was pretty much a natural response for them. They were blood thirsty and generally aggressive towards all races and after they had wiped out all of the enemy they turned on itself. This was a fierce and savage thing with very few left alive, it was a fierce instinct that the Linsani were struggling to keep a lid on. They were finding that the Dark Talon was too fierce to be used competently.

They're survival instincts were too much to be used competently. And nine times out of ten they wiped themselves out. I mean this could be used as an advantage and it was win, win. But they were trying keep control of the Talon. And this was becoming more and more difficult. But still they were trying to enhance the biological makeup of the xenomorph. Not that it wasn't deadly and fast enough. No, it had excelled in ferocious and fast behaviour but they just couldn't control it to its full potential, leaving only one option for the Talon and that was annihilation. This is why it was more often than not they had to go back to the drawing board and fuse DNA of the Talon with other life forms. Mainly genetically enhanced scorpions. And other lethal bugs. The creature was easy to create yet difficult to control. As most of them were giving over to an insatiable hunger which took over each Talon, which after killing and tearing apart the enemy their hunger was all consuming and all inducing their habit that was death and a feeding frenzy. After it consumed the enemy, it had nothing more than the option to consume each other. This was ingrained in their DNA and was taking up all the time of the Linsani Biological weapons division. They knew it was possible as first tests using electric collars but this in the end drove them wilder, more destructive and the pain from the electric collars just fuelled their hunger for food and mayhem. This was all trial and error and they would have some positive results then have to destroy what was left, this left the Linsani with little or no method of control with the dark talon, so often they had to destroy the species. It was the only way to control the xenomorph.

The Reapers were watching a video of the Dark Talons early trials on certain space stations that were deemed as havens for the deserters of the Imperium. They sat and watched as they floated through space towards one of the dens of deserters. Then the action as the Talon ripped a huge hole into the hull of the station. Then the camera's flipped to the destruction of the ex-Troopers, as they tore through metal, destroying Troopers, a hand full at a time. Dayton laughed a little and said as the Dark Talons assault drew to an end. "We got problems!"

The rest murmured and said, "Then some".

Tiris carried on his study in the Dark Talon, Then when he had finished watching all the footage and studying all the Biological charts looking for a weakness, he smiled and said to himself, "Comes to us all".

He then lit another stogie and carried on studying the movements of the Dark Talon. Cascoe sent another encoded message to Tiris asking for help and assuming the Dark Talon had a weakness.

Tiris responded, "The Dark Talon are totally immune to most energy weapons their hides thick and dense".

"They must have a weakness?" asked Cascoe.

"The best weapon we have to throw at them are our SMG's with splitter ammunition".

Cascoe sighed. "I take it they still haven't found a way to control them?"

Tiris Laughed, "Control something that chaotic, no they don't have a clue".

Cascoe smiled and hissed, "Lovely fucking war this."

Tiris spoke about other things, mundane little things. They grew to have quite the rapport with each other. Tiris finished flicked the comm links off and carried on looking over the biological data on the Dark Talon. He was sure he was missing something. But couldn't put his finger on it, he kept on studying, watching how easily it was for the Dark Talon to rip through metal and I'm talking ten fifteen inches thick. Their claws tore holes like a warm knife through butter. Then they boarded and first kill was a glorious one.

Where the rest of the Dark Talon were fast at devouring the two or three first kills then they carried on. Ripping walls like cardboard. And again they devoured after destroying most of the local deserters who all had the K seventy eight armour and high calibre and mass destructive plasma and other energy weapons. The ones that were making a decent stand were the ones with the small SMG carbines, loaded with splitter, armour piercing rounds. But it expended a lot of rounds to put down one of the Dark Talon. That was a major drawback. But Tiris was sure there was something he was missing, something amidst the feeding frenzy.

They had a single purpose, and that was to kill and eat. They couldn't be stopped and the more you flung at them the angrier they got. The more powerful they became they were ripping apart three or four Storm Troopers at a time and there was very little they could do to stop them. As I said, it took a lot of splitter rounds to quell the Dark Talon and send it into Hell. But they seemed to get braver and bolder as the Troopers ammunition diminished and Hand to hand against the xenomorph, well if they had the K eleven armour maybe, they would have a chance. But it still remained their domination and showed that they had nothing to lose as they were acting on instinct. Kill, feed, kill, feed. Then they would finish their carnage, and begin to feed, not just on the Troopers but their own kind as well.

Lasers and other tech weapons seemed to glance and ricochet off the Dark Talons hide. They were pretty much invulnerable. Tiris switched off the video and turned off the Genetic and bio charts for the Dark Talon.

"Okay Trooper's we got a short mission to go on, then we will discuss the Dark Talons".

They all checked in. The *Defiant* then headed off to the Rygon five to pick up a cargo of Paradox. Then they would head back to the Orion system, drop off the cargo collect the gold credits then head away to the Orgis system and watch how badly ravaged the system was getting in the continuation of the Faith Wars. The Trill were putting up one hell of a fight. But the Titan Reaper squad was decimating most of the Trill home guard. And, on the other hand the Dark Talon were making short work of the Trill's home guard.

The Medusa seed was now obsolete and the Trill were working on a few tricks of their own. One in particular was the Trills best, it was the lightning weapon that had been super enhanced. It was pretty thorough and was decimating the Storm Troopers that went up against the Trill who had worked on it as they knew the only way to get ahead was to somehow make the Linsani dampener switch useless and this may tip the scales in the Trills favour. It may even give them an edge against the Titan Reapers. But alas they had run aground with its use on the Dark Talon. It was useless against them didn't work at all. But still the field was open for them, and they had technicians working on biological counter weapons funnily enough similar to the Medusa Seed. But it was moving slowly and several steps behind in the glory fight, the Faith Wars carried on.

The Trill holding out as a barrage after barrage of Talon and Troopers smashed into the Trills home System. The fight was bloody and vicious with the Titan reapers really appearing to have all the cards, they moved with sureness and were methodical in their art of war. Each one with nothing to lose. But plenty to prove. The armour gave them a Godlike existence and they lapped it up, worshiped and made themselves as no one else could take their place, Tiris was growling at the sight as the chaos ensued on the battle front. The Titans and Talon were showing just what kind of race the humans were. Selfish annihilators, who didn't give a damn about anyone other than themselves. They wouldn't rest until the Trill were on the edge of extinction then they may take them as slaves and rule the Universe with utter surety.

Tiris punched in the target's in the distance a battleship that was apparently having a good time destroying Trill escape pods from one of its warcraft. The *Defiant* sent the ship that was called Titus a message saying that they would like to join in the carnage. The *Titus* extended its honorary position thinking the more the merrier. The *ESP* broke away from the *Defiant* and began to sweep with radar to see if any of the Trill were alive.

They had been decimated and not a single Trill soldier had survived. Bucker shouted through the hail and barrage and started to attack the *Titus*. The *Defiant* did the same, Tiris was equally as pissed as Bucker. They had come to like the catlike Trill knowing that the majority of them were a simple calm people. But humans being selfish and cruel in nature had to rule and destroy anything they didn't understand. It was a part of the existence that no one could understand, the human race.

The *Defiant* locked on to the *Titus* with its plasma cannon and began to blast at the battle cruiser. The *Defiant* aimed again at the engineer level with nuclear sidewinders. These blasted the front end of the cruiser. It was over before it really started. And Tiris and Bucker both acknowledge the fact if there was one thing they knew what to do and that was to get even. They flew by the burning wreckage of the human battlecruiser. And the Troopers on the *Titus* were left floating out in the icy cavernous area known as space.

"Now that was fun," said Bucker.

Tiris smiled puffed away and said, "That was a pleasure". They then headed back towards the Trill home worlds and hoped to meet up with Cascoe.

"Kat man du, this is rip cord". Tiris was use to the time between the two of them contacting each other so he repeated, "Kat man Du This is rip cord do you copy?"

Cascoe answered but the urgency in his voice said it all. "Yes Rip Cord I copy. I'm just in a bit of a situation at the moment".

Tiris let out a sigh as if to say, "Here we go again? Is there anything we can do to help Kat man Du?"

Cascoe replied after a brief static array. "We need help, most of our reinforcements are spent just trying to hold back the sheer ferocious assault, yes we need help".

Tiris locked in on the warcrafts location and set the craft for hyper space. They would be there in a matter of hours. The ship purged and cleaned the Ion field, where they needed to go was not too distant, they had plenty of nuclear atomic energy so Tiris smiled to himself and thought 'I hope we get to you on time Kat man Du?' "Hang in there Kats we'll be there soon". Tiris flicked the shifter into auto and went and donned his K eleven Power armour, the rest of the reaper squads did the same letting the urgency settle in.

"I just hope we get there in time," said Artemis, as the armour powered round him.

"What are we facing sir?" asked Hue.

"Well if it has got Cascoe on the ropes then it must be formidable," said Tiris.

The rest of the reaper squads powered up. They would reach that particular nebula in a short while. They slowed down just short of the carnage, It was Talon and they were swarming all over the Warcraft. Tearing the ship to pieces. And devouring the Trill as if they had been fed when at their hungriest. This was the most carnage the Reapers had seen with the Talon. They had watched on film and disk the Talon tear into Troopers this was different, They were more aggressive more animalistic. They were devouring and ripping into the Trill soldiers, and blood and guts were everywhere. Entrails were floating as the Talon ripped and bit into the Kat like race.

We are going to have to Nuke them. Bucker climbed into the pilot seat and ready the small craft for a brutal assault. The *ESP* hummed as the engines began to kick in, Tiris and the rest of the reaper squads went and sat in las cannon seats and two other Reapers manned the Nuclear sidewinder missiles. They began their assault on the dark Talon. Bucker swung by a group of Talon who were feeding fresh. He fired off two missiles at what looked to be three or four of the Xenomorphs. This was the best they were going to get. And it wasn't going to get that easy again. No that was, mercy compared to what Bucker had in store for them. He began to charge up the Ion cannon and the Laser cannons. He would do a tunnel sweep and try to get at the heart of the Talon. He began to blast and pick off the Talon as he headed to the heart of the Xenomorphs. They were swarming all over the main deck of the Warcraft. Every now and then there was a scream as a Trill soldier was ripped to pieces. Then Bucker really got angry and started to fire off on the Talon, destroying them and leaving a cloud of vapour. The ash that was left turned pitch black and looked like the entrails of a black hole. He carried on as did the *Defiant* and they were really making headway. The only problem was the comm link between Tiris and Cascoe was cut out they were in total radio silence. With nothing but static.

They couldn't even communicate using morse code as the Talon had wiped out the wire tracer. Bucker carried on destroying the Xenomorphs. Knowing that after a while their morale would be shaken and they would be facing the inevitable. Death. The chaos the mayhem, the devastation. The sure fire reason for a species to become scared was when the majority of their HIVE was dead leaving very few to keep on going, this was a turning point in the history of the Marches, They had proved combat effectiveness with the Talon losing a sure fire position of power with savagery. No, it was brains versus animalistic power and brains showed more than willing, more like a strength of power that can only come from a militant mind. And Bucker was a seasoned veteran in the Martial world. He had proven himself a valuable asset and this was never thrown out the window so to speak.

He didn't have the pride of a fool either no he was cool calm and collected. And Tiris wouldn't operate with another. No he had deliberately searched for the right aptitudes and Bucker had just shown the qualities of a regal lion. And this could not be denied. They only had one more thing to do and that was board the war craft and see to the wounded Trill. But this was a task and a deadly destructive one at that. They came up next to the air dock and docked. Then they prepared to board and knew that what they were about to face was extremely dangerous and could not be underestimated.

The armour they had on was strong and very versatile. They each had a SMG carbine loaded with splitter rounds as this was the only round that had produced results. No they were ready for the Talon and it was going to be no picnic. So they powered up their armour, lock and loaded their carbines and entered the war craft. They were on high alert but had a lot to be thankful for, they knew that the Talon would be waiting closer to the main deck, were the majority of the Talon had honed in on. The craft was short circuiting all over and there was little light in the ship, they were cautious and kept themselves vigilant. They made an encounter near the engine room of the craft. The Talon was feasting on a dead Trill soldier when Dayton came across it. The crunch of bone and sickening ripping of flesh as the Talon feasted. He aimed his weapon and let off the full magazine. It struck the Xenomorph and ripped its back open with small explosions as the splitter rounds exploded. Ripping the creature apart. The thing screeched as it was torn apart, and the clear viscous bug like blood gushed through the wounds and made a pool at the feet of Dayton.

The Reaper squad were on high alert knowing these things were cunning and hungry. Dayton and the rest of them were cautious and headed towards the main deck. They encountered a few of them but nothing they couldn't handle. It was as if they had decided to dissipate. And leave the rest for what came next.

"Yep!" said Dayton, "It's quiet".

Samster made a comment, "Yeah too quiet".

They then continued into the main deck of the warcraft. The feeding frenzy had suddenly abated, and the rest of the Xenomorph had left. Even Tiris found the lack of hostiles too spooky, "Nobody do anything heroic," said Tiris. They then after an alarmingly lack of resistance they found Cascoe and a whole heap of dead bugs. But he had managed to wipe out six or seven of them before turning his weapon on himself. He blew the back of his feline skull all over the wall. Tiris turned his head the picture wasn't pretty. He sighed into his comm link and said, "The best friend I had".

"Okay lads we got to scuttle her and leave nothing but dust." They all checked in then walked off into the crafts derelict and bloody tomb. This was getting to be a habit of Tiris. First the Linsani station and now one of his only friends. He didn't have many but the ones he had were like gold dust, especially Cascoe.

They set the charges on the fusion and Ion propulsion unit in the engineering section on the warcraft. Then they all boarded the *Defiant* and flew off into space. Just as they made safe distance the warcraft grew into a bright light then sent a shock wave so large it almost turned out the lights on the *Defiant*. They then headed back towards the Orion nebula to refuel and get more ammunition and more rockets. Especially for the *ESP*.

Bucker came down onto deck smiled sadly and said, "Sorry about Cascoe".

Tiris blew on his match that he had just struck to light his stogie. "Yep hell of a thing losing a brother in arms. Especially one that was more kin than you ever thought he was".

Bucker sneered and replied, "It's the loss, it wears on a man especially in these trying times".

Tiris nodded and puffed away on his stogie. They had three more sleep cycles until back in the Orion Nebula.

Chapter Seventeen

Taxus was reading the report on the Dark Talon and its success. He smiled as the numbers were good, this was the best weapon that the LInsani technicians had brought for war. I mean now that the Medusa Seed was inert, he was running out of options, but the Dark Talon was proving to be a serious class a weapon. The xenomorph had a flaw and that was its hunger. But rending the Talon inert had been difficult and usually they had to nuke the site of the Dark Talon.

This was greeted with a great sullen silence before the action was taken. But they couldn't run the risk of the Dark Talon roaming free. So nuclear annihilation was the only course they had to use. And the Imperium battlecruisers did so vigilantly. It was a win, win situation. And saved a lot of Storm Troopers lives (Well the ones that managed to jump ship before the Nukes were used). The rest an expendable asset. Taxus carried on reading the success rate of the Talon. They had finally turned a corner in the Faith Wars and they knew it was worth the destruction that they had to use. The use of weapons of mass destruction after the Dark Talon had destroyed the enemy was seen as just another day in the war. And it was no big thing. With whole planets being torn asunder with the Talon being a force that couldn't be quelled. Couldn't be stopped, just the perfect killing machines. No conscience, no way of stopping them. They were being grown in DNA tanks in the Linsani system of space. They were fast breeders as well and replenished numbers quickly. But still they had no restraint in the xenomorph. They were looking into a chemical enzyme that sent them into a slow sullen sleep. But this was only trial and had a major drawback, and that was, it sometimes killed the Talon. And this was a major drawback. But enhancements were being discovered every day. And the Talon was becoming more and more deadly, being a force that was formidable and extremely deadly.

Tiris smiled as they docked on the Space station in the Orion system. He thought about the past results with the Talon and wondered if there was some sort of genetic weapon they could use against the Talon. A nerve gas or poison liquid. Some sort of acid that could be weaponised. He thought that the local Tech heads were needed to look into said weapons. He would do this after getting more ammo and fuel. They would then begin to look into destructive pathogens and liquid weapons. Of course they would have to capture a hive of xenomorphs and test the weapons. But that was easier said than done. He began to formulate a plan. And he called Bucker into the Bridge.

Bucker looked around and sniffed. "Is everything alright sir?"

Tiris smiled and replied, "I'm brainstorming sergeant".

Bucker carried on looking around the Bridge looking at the various monitors and 3d molecular break downs of the Talon. But he knew that it just wasn't that simple with the Talon. No he had his hands full with the way the Xenomorph attacked and devoured. It was a study that would be very meticulous and detailed. The fact that the Talon could tear through sheet metal like it was wet paper. But that was just the tip of the iceberg. No he had a lot to consider. Especially the ferocity of the Talon. They seemed to fight without having to reenergise, they were constantly eating as they destroyed. They were high in metabolism and quick to regenerate. Their hide was thick and tough with a beetle like structure that was super impenetrable. Most weapons ricochet off the dark hide.

"Now Bucker I need an idea on how to capture a hive of Dark Talon."

Bucker smiled, "It won't be fucking easy," he replied.

Tiris snorted, "Well, we need all the input we can get".

Bucker placed his skull helmet on the computer console. "Yes sir"

Tiris looked on at the carnage of a test setting where several Trill were faced head on with the Dark Talon. They were ripped and devoured by a small hive of at least twelve xenomorph. They had no chance. They only had their bare hands and the high octane martial arts that came with the training of Trill soldiers, no they had no chance. They were useless. Tiris was particularly shocked by the strength of the Talon. They made the act seem as though it was as easy as breathing. It was ingrained in them the violence, the aggression. The hunger. Tiris dismissed Bucker who went about his duties that included re-fuelling and re-arming the *Defiant* and the *ESP*.

Tiris smiled at the monitors that held the carnage of the Talon, he was close and he knew it, no he was getting that satisfied feeling of uncovering the secret pathogen that may swing this war back in the favour of the Trill. This was still a long way off but he knew that he was making progress. Tiris downloaded the various pathogens and weaponized that held the most potential for a complete destruction of a full hive. He then set foot on the Orion station and went straight to the Tech Heads. He smiled as the head tech chief greeted him at the front of his laboratory. He handed the disc to the Lead Technician.

He smiled and said, "Fun and Games, huh."

Tiris smiled and replied, "How long is this going to take?"

The man in the white lab shirt smiled and said, "a couple of days, but that depends on how much intel there is on the Talon."

Tiris looked around, the lab technician carried on, "We still need a Hive to test the various weapons on".

Tiris went, "Hmm that's going to be tricky. As the majority of them are in the Linsani region of space".

The technician smiled and said, "I'm sure you will think of something."

Tiris looked around again then took the man's hand and said, "I'll sort something out. I mean if anything we are adaptable". He then turned and walked away. Back to the *Defiant*.

Bucker was loading the last of the missiles and ammunition, while the rest of the reaper squads were loading up on provisions. "We have to wait a couple of day's so as not to leave you in the dark we really have our work cut out"

The Squads gave a small murmur and Tiris, "We got to catch and hold a full-on Hive of Talon".

The Squad murmured again.

"I know, I know we aren't tough enough". He then let out a small laugh and continued. "But it's not just about us, it's about our friends who are coming up against the Talon" He then said, "so check in if you are willing to risk it all for peace and sovereignty?"

They all checked in, hell they didn't have anything else to do. And to most of them it was just the kind of thing that they were trained for. It was a challenge and it was a good challenge at that. They finished stocking up supplies and went and got themselves some sleep. It was going to be a long couple of days whilst they waited for the outcome on the way to deal with the Talon. But this was only preliminary as they still had to test the Pathogens and weapons on a Hive. The two days crawled in a boring and slow manor. But they played cards and did a little gambling. Polished up on their hand-to-hand combat. This passed the cycles away. Then the Technician called Tiris.

"Sir I have a lead on two possible pathogens, ones a nerve agent the other a gas that breaks down the Talons hide and leaves then vulnerable to normal weapons".

Tiris smiled and said, "I knew I was onto something".

The technician smiled, "I still need a Hive to try out the weapons".

Tiris laughed, "we're on it man, ye of little faith".

The Technician laughed, "That may be but don't get yourself killed trying to capture one".

Tiris laughed and strapped himself into his chair.

"Right Troopers strap in we're going on a bug hunt".

They all did as he said and the Ion propulsion engine purged itself and the shot off into space heading for the

Linsani Space region. The *Defiant* began to scan around for mobile space stations that were housing Hive's of Dark Talon. They scanned a full day and night and nothing, not even a small carrier ship. No, they had lucked out on the Linsani Factor. They would have to get closer to one of the Linsani Home worlds. And that meant showing themselves. To the high guard in the local vicinity. That wasn't what they needed. So Tiris carried on scanning the local system hoping he would pick up the signs of a space laboratory. And just as they were about to call it a day, they noticed a small skiff towing a large ship with all kinds of things on board.

Tiris grinned and said through the comm link, "We have a winner".

Everybody prepare for docking and rocking the ship. They docked on the primary air lock on the Skiff. Then Tiris and Reaper team one, captured the Skiff and its crew with very little opposition. Tiris threw the captain and his two navigational pilots into the *Defiant*'s Brigg. They then sped off back to Orion. It turned out they had captured not just one hive but three. Tiris was proud of his squad of Reapers and showed so by having a little gathering where each of the Reapers was given a cigar and a bottle of alcohol of their choice. They celebrated as they knew that this was just the result they needed. It meant shutting down the Imperium's deadliest weapon. This was going their way. They arrived at the Orion Nebula and docked with the Skiff coming right up behind the *Defiant*. Tiris sent a direct message to the Technicians on the Orion station. They were greeted by about seventeen Tech's all ahhing and cooing over the acquisition of the Hives.

"We were lucky," said Tiris to the tech head.

He replied, "That's a fucking massive Jackpot".

Tiris humphed and said, "Like I said we was lucky". They then began the testing of nerve agents and gasses. "This will take a while and I mean a while".

Tiris shrugged his shoulders and said, "whatever man, we aren't in a rush."

The head Tech smiled and began to dress in his anti-contamination suit. As did several of the other Tech heads. The team then spotted the first hive via an AI link with a remote bot. They switched on the carbon freeze and began to remove the deadly pupeios in their frozen state, then they began to warm the thing up in all their glory. They didn't wait a second for the thing to begin producing deadly bugs, no they blasted it with the Medusa Hybrid gas which had startling effects on the thing. It disintegrated most of the Xeno shell that protected and nurtured it. The things molecular DNA began to liquidise and break down into goo.

The team carried on with more tests on the second and third HIVE. Some test with the nerve agent was conducted and it showed promise, not as clean as the Medusa Hybrid but it was close to finishing of by implosion, the insides swelling yet solidifying at the same time. This led to the explosion in the Hive's major abdomen. This sent entrails and organs clear across the fifty-foot room. But this was just not good enough. No they needed the first Gas to be total annihilation. And then some, they came up against another hurdle, the Hive was functioning on more than a cellular level no it was regenerating from the bass primordial goo to the hardened xenomorph that was the Talon. It was somehow regenerating to its full cellular level, this was done with bone sickening crunching and scraping its claws and rest of its form together. The Talon was quickly adapting to its, environment. Using it to its advantage. The techs were quick in their studies knowing that the things heart was a major factor in its re-birth. The thing had a black as coal heart and it beat around about twice the time of a human heart. The techs started for the third Hive, again freezing the Bug then waking it up slowly. This time they would use the liquid acid on its hide.

The stuff was like the foam out of a fire extinguisher, it quickly bound onto the xenomorph. Then said thing began to liquidise and melt to waterlike substance. The Tech called it flushing and said it was the best result so far. The Talon had no way of surviving the foam. And said weapon was easy to make and cost little to produce. But the foam was unstable and sometimes split and was useless. But the Tech assured Tiris that this was a temporary setback and would be easy to fix. The Tech's had done well and Tiris couldn't deny this. 'In fact they had excelled in their task' He thought.

The first weapon was a go, the second weapon was a miss, but the third weapon was well a clear on go, but they had to work out the kinks in the foam. Tiris was well impressed. They sent a code nine secret message to the Trill High Guard with the chemical formula of both the foam and the Gas. The Trill were happy to receive the weapons this would put them back in the game in the Faith Wars. Tiris smiled and gathered as many of the two weapons as he could. He then headed back on to the *Defiant* and began his departure into the Faith Wars, he had major payback to deal out with his Squads of Reapers. He was formulating a plan. He would call in the favours he had with Guardian

Angel, Kurt Lidel. Then he would get in contact with Tooms and his band of Pirates. Then they would show up on the Linsani Home world, where they would show there initiative and destroy as many Hives as they could.

'This was gonna be fun' thought Tiris.

Chapter Eighteen

Taxus was doing his ceremonial executions. Four in total, he was feeling good within himself. He grimaced as he shot the fourth one, then settled down as the bodies were taking away to harvest their organs for medical purposes. This was the only compassionate thing he did. But he didn't let that lose him any sleep. He was having guests that night and it was as usual a sordid affair between him and three or four young boys whom he would choke in front of his guests, the guests compiled of a tax inspector and three Generals from his Naval forces. They never complained, knew all about the man's deviant behaviour but knew they valued their lives even more. The families of the boys were sold into slave labour, made to work in the paradox refineries, where they were told that if they even breathed a word they would be skinned alive and sent to a prison world to suffer for their last days. They would then be used as food for the inmates of said world.

So no, nobody had the guts to complain. He gathered his things as he headed to the dining room where he would begin his festivities. He was smiling, not the smile of a content man, not the smile of a homicidal Tyrant that was used to getting his own way. Nobody even whispered against Taxus as his rule was supreme and somebody was always willing to cut the throat of anyone else, so as to get themselves more gold Credits. This is why he did the brutal show of strength to his generals and ministers. He was also fond of the feeling of power that coursed through his veins, the adrenaline, the dopamine, he knew that there was no better rush especially when you mixed it with Paradox and wine. And if you think he laughed at the act, only when no one else was around. And even then if you heard him laughing you got out the way. It was a foreboding sound that made your skin crawl and sent a sense of unease and panic through your body.

No Taxus was evil incarnate and he took pride in his psychosis that had left the charts long ago. He was sinister and creepy. You just had to look at him and see that the robes, the gold only gave the man a more squeaky clean importance. But it was shallow, it was twisted. his eyes were mad and wild and he was constantly staring into the dark distance. And the scarred psyche that he had was permanently twisting leaving his soul in the regions of despair. And that was why he committed such horrible atrocities. He never made excuses for himself as he knew they would be paper thin. And would cause people to judge him. No his fate and fortune were sealed, he was now head in the Imperium and could continue to commit the treacherous and lecherous acts that he had somehow thought were normal. I mean he needed to commit these atrocities it was the only way he could breathe air without needing to report to anyone.

People still looked up to him. They were families of Troopers who were assured rank and privileges and there was a lot of Troopers that stayed loyal. But, the Generals and ministers hid the true soul of the Emperor.

His darkness was never ever found out, it was hushed at the pain of death. And every now and then someone stumbled onto Taxus's dark, deviant and sinister side. He was as said, evil incarnate.

Chapter Nineteen

Tiris sat back as the *Defiant* sped off towards the Linsani worlds. The Dark Talon was being housed on a couple of worlds and on a couple of space stations. They were modifying them and housing them in large space cruisers that housed at least a hundred hives per ship. Each hive was split into eight or nine of the Xenomorph bugs. They were six feet tall with black Talons that were as strong as at least twenty men strong. There hide was similar to a scorpions but tougher. They were indestructible and could not be fended off. But Tiris smiled as he looked at the gas and foam. There was enough to wipe out the planets that housed them they would swoop over the surface and lay a large blanket of the foam on the Dark Talon. Then they would affix a pipe into the space station's and gassed the rest of them. After they had finished off one of the Planets, they sealed the deal with a megaton nuclear bomb. This was all she wrote. Tooms and Kurt began to finish off the cruisers, with foam and gas.

The Linsani were neither ready nor in control of the attack. Some of them managed to speed off into the marches darkest space. They were lucky, but Tiris had plans for them after the chemical campaign had finished. Tiris smiled and enjoyed his Stogie. As the megaton bomb wiped out the Dark Talon with surety. They had great success with both the foam and the gas. But the Nuke that was just to reassure them that they had a foothold in this war.

Tiris was a renegade of true destructive power and now he held all the aces, the only thing that was causing him a mild annoyance was the Titan Reaper squads. But he was sure that this was only a minor headache. But it was there and dangerously so. He got the squads to check in just to make sure. Tiris smiled as the last of them checked in, then he flipped the switch and headed back to the Orion nebula.

Taxus smashed up his ornately decorated bed chamber. Nobody stopped him, he was wild, he killed two servants in the process. No that wasn't the news he wanted to hear.

"The destruction of the Dark Talon sealed and delivered by Tiris and his Reapers". Taxus was roaring a deep throaty thunderous noise that put the chill up his servants and several squads of Storm Troopers. And these were seasoned professional Troopers, they had done mission after mission. But still Taxus unnerved them as they boarded their battlecruiser and took up combat seating. One of them said to the other, "Jeeze he's pissed."

The Trooper adjusted his mask, "That'll be the Reapers having the final say on the Dark Talon".

"I think the fight will be more equal without the bugs" The First trooper said.

The second Trooper smiled darkly to himself, "It's more like a battle without the Dark Talon and that suites me fine," He answered.

They then prepared for the oncoming onslaught. They were after all still at war with the Trill.

Tiris smiled as they docked with the Orion space station, everybody was whooping and hollering as Tiris opened the hatch. They grabbed him and gave him a royal hoist. They knew that it was the only thing to expect from Tiris and his two squads of Reapers. I mean they were legends in their own right. This was a major win for humanity and Trill alike. The Faith Wars were about fizzle themselves out. As a lock of stalemate was becoming more and more likely, the two forces making it only just and no more.

They locked in their interstellar combat, with both proving to each other that they were a force to be reckoned with. They held their death lock, both the General and the Warlord poising at the edge of mass destruction. They were clear and just had to flick the switch and interstellar nuclear warheads would hit each other. They poised and the whole of the Marches held their breath. Knowing the two races were on an equal par with each other, but neither of them having the guts to flick the kill switch and carry through with nuclear annihilation. Tiris watched the two armadas as they carried on the stalemate. He knew that the two of them were at each-others mercy. No they weren't, yes he knew it, neither would back down then he heard the loud shrill as the two of them fired their nukes. There was a huge flash of light as the two sides directed their weapons at each other. Then the whole of the marches rumbled as the megaton weapons went off. That was the last stand for the two of them, both I guess as they had lost faith in the Faith Wars.

"Fucking sin," said Tiris then switched the monitor off. He smiled as he had seen this coming. "Now I deal with you Taxus," said Tiris,

He then gathered his two squads of Reapers told them that this was the last mission. The last mission and it wasn't going to be easy. Apart from the countless Storm Troopers that they would have to contend with, they also had the Reaper Titans to deal with. And they had no hope of the Titans changing sides.

Tiris smiled as they flew through the system to end at the Imperium's strong hold Becrest. They were bang on time, as the Troopers were all dead at the last stand. But still Tiris grimaced more as he got close to the strong hold. This was going to be challenging, Being as they were only sixteenth in strength. But this was only a small matter. And Tiris had never backed down from a good old-fashioned battle. And this would be a true test. The Titans had superior strength and superior armour. He would rely on tactics to out manoeuvre the large bulky Titans. But speed wasn't the only thing they had, no they had clarity and vision. A combination that would see them through this test. No Tiris was ready for this battle, he was grimacing all the way with his stogie lit and a chance to fight. Bucker was resting in the *ESP* waiting for the orders. Then he would detach from piggy backing the *Defiant* and into full combat mode.

Chapter Twenty

Taxus was waiting for his Generals to take him off world, He was just about ready when the attack was reported. "Sire?" Came the voice over the comm's unit, "Sire" It said again.

"Yes what is it?" He replied.

The voice came through again, "We need to move you like immediately".

Taxus snorted, "Don't take too long," he said. Then the first of the nukes hit the Stronghold. Taxus felt the ground shake beneath his feet.

'They aint pulling there punches,' Thought Taxus. He then issued the order to fire back at the *Defiant* and its crew. But the Becrest had one failing and that was the armour around the centre of the Stronghold was weaker than the rest of the Stronghold. Taxus was being rushed to the Imperial escape ship. The Titans took up positions as he was being rushed away from the Becrest. Again the rumble through out the Stronghold. He was getting nervous and started to complain at the length of time it was taking for them to leave.

They punched in the coordinates then shot off into space, heading for Terra. They would be there in six or seven hours. Blind luck saved the Emperor that day, but the fight wasn't over. No, Tiris had a plan to destroy the Becrest stronghold and he knew the Titans were in that stronghold somewhere probably close to the Imperial High throne. Tiris landed gently just outside the Becrests main door. Just as he did this he watched as the Escape ship shot out of its hiding place and out into space. The reapers disembarked from the *Defiant* and started to run a by-pass for the front entrance. The door whirred then the dead bolts opened and the door slid to the left side. They took up flanking positions on either side of the gigantic metal door. The plasma cannons were at front whilst the rest of them followed up the rear. The light was in red alert so everything was bathed in red. But this caused little problem to the Reapers. They then encountered their first Titan. It was laying in wait just off to the right of Reaper Team one.

It struck and struck hard. Sending a volley of laser beams at the front gunner who was unaware he had been hit until the flashed at him and glided off his suit, "Duster here first hostile has just struck." He then checked himself and made sure he wasn't wounded and that his armour wasn't rent. Tiris responded a couple of seconds later. "Return fire soldier."

Duster started immediately to aim the high energy weapon at the Titan then as the Plasma rifle gained energy he fired three large bursts of molten laser. Two of them hit the Titan and one hit the wall. The Titans armour which was double the strength of the Reapers K eleven armour. He took the hits and carried on sending volley after volley of sporadic laser beams. The Reaper team managed to survive but soon realised they were pinned by the large Titan. They carried on fighting the Titan, whilst in the throes of war Dayton sent forth several spider mines to the feet of the Titan. He didn't even notice until Dayton pressed the Kill switch and blew the legs away from the Titan. They then got the opportunity to see how much damage they could take before being destroyed. They circled the heavily armoured Trooper and threw everything they had at it. They began to buckle its armour after about three minutes of open fire and that included the Plasma weapons. But after another two minutes they had it destroyed and blood puddled out of the armoured Storm Trooper.

He was dead. The Troopers all laughed as the man died. They then checked the armour out and Dayton said, "See not so tough".

They laughed again. Tiris sighed and said, "Such is war,"

They then headed further into the Stronghold. The next opponent was a group of lack lustre Storm Troopers who soon as they saw the Reapers they decided to join the reapers. They flung their arms in the air and said, "Sorry sir we aren't in this fight". The statement was a cold motherfucking fact. And Tiris couldn't blame the Storm Troopers. So they strapped them against the engine coolant pipes and disarmed them. They then walked away and all that squad of Storm Troopers could hear was the Reapers joking and laughing.

But the captain shrugged and said, "Nothing I can do lads maybe they will show us mercy and take us on board the *Defiant*?" That question hung their as if it was a standing joke. Tiris joined in the laughter. Then all of a sudden, he grew uneasy. And knew something was waiting just past the mess hall. They split up at the junction that led to the mess hall and his imperial sleeping quarters. Dayton took a team down the junction heading towards the Imperial sleeping chambers. While Tiris proceeded with caution down to the mess hall. He knew something wasn't right, he had this uncanny ability to know when things were about to go south on him and it usually meant bloodily so. He switched on his skulls helmet targeting scanner. And swept the large room that was unoccupied.

"I smell a rat boys," They all switched their targeting functions on. Tiris knew that the man Piper who was taking point with his large plasma thrower would be ready for anything that was flung at him. Tiris knew his men like the back of his hand, trusted them with the patience of a saint. And knew they were loyal to him and no amount of money would see them betray Tiris.

Just after the sweep was done by Tiris and the rest of his Reapers thought, 'This is easy, this is to easy'. They were suddenly hit with blinding light and the concussion of several small grenades. They had just walked into a Titan trap. Then the titan Reapers began to shoot electric dampers, at the crew of Reapers. That which would stop all functions on the Reaper teams. But they were suddenly encroached by the other team who had come up from the rear of the mess hall. They began by blowing the legs out of two of them with the spider mines, then the other three, who were too busy trying to incapacitate the other eleven, were suddenly going down to spider mines and heavy SMG carbine fire with splitter rounds.

Dayton was smiling as the explosions of his were dead on target. Whereas the Titans couldn't gain any exposure on who was controlling the spider mines.

The fact was he smelt that cheesy trap a mile away. So as he had split from the *Defiant* team, once he had an unusual smile on his face as if to say okay you think you've got us sussed. But no sweethearts. I got youse sussed. He heard them moving through to the mess hall and heard the orders to concuss them with flash and deep demolition charges. They were only trying to capture Tiris, and through all things that had happened that wasn't what was going to happen.

Like I said Dayton smelt that cheese eating trap. And boy was Tiris glad to see Dayton pull up the rear. And waste the Titans. See, one thing that Tiris' Reapers had that the Titans didn't was that was they were more mobile had more speed and more agility. That was a major factor in this battle. Oh, the Titans were smart, but too smart, to cocky, they relied on brute force. Whereas the two Reaper teams they were up against were all highly decorated special forces who had seen more than their fair share of the Faith Wars. But that was all she wrote about the Titans, the rest of them were guarding the Emperor Taxus on his way back to Terra.

Tiris and Bucker began to set nuclear charges on the Imperial Strong hold Becrest. They then boarded The *Defiant* and headed away as the clock ticked away the last few seconds of whoever was still in that stronghold. The charges blasted the stronghold to oblivion.

Tiris punched in the coordinates to the Orgis System. Looking to meet up with an emissary of the Trill seeing as Cascoe was dead. The Emperor would wait for another day and that would be his final day in this universe. Tiris sent the coded message to the Trill High Guard. Hoping for a final settlement on the destruction of the Dark Talon. But the real prize was in finding and finishing the Emperor. It was a sixty billion credit reward from the Trill and other investor's it staked up to be one hundred billion Gold credits. Enough to buy your own little system of worlds and start to civilise the planet's. It was everybody's little dream. But you had to kill the Emperor first and that was nigh on impossible. But, Tiris was just waiting. Keeping cool, he knew that there was one certainty and that before everything happened it would be him or Taxus that would be dead.

Tiris waited in dead space for the return message from the Trill. He was a very patient man especially when it came to the politics of war. He smiled and flicked the match he had lit then blew a big exhale of smoke. The return message came a sleep cycle away and it was a congratulation for their handling of the Stronghold Becrest.

"Well done sir," came the feline voice of the principle war lord of the Trill.

"It was their mistake," came the gruff voice of the Colonel. "They should never have given me this armour".

The feline voice purred and responded, "I am Acentua, The new Warlord of the Trill".

Tiris liked him already. "Well Acentua we have a small yet much deserved fee for the destruction of the Talon?"

Acentua purred some more, "Yes you do, yes you do".

He then sent coordinates for them to meet at the farthest end of the Orgis system. They then sped off to meet each other. Tiris was all boosted up to meet the replacement for Cascoe. He was fairly confident that the Trill Warlord felt the same as him. So he wasn't out to prove anything to the Trill Warlord.

They met two days later at an abandoned outpost at the farthest away point of the Orgis System. They shook and gripped each-others wrists. Then had a nice meal and some wine They discussed the way and shape of the universe as it was now seeing the end of the Faith Wars. Acentua proved that his friendship with Tiris was a stable and healthy one they began to discuss tactics on getting the Emperor Taxus to either commit suicide or render himself to the Trill High Guard in which case he would be executed. Tiris thought of both scenarios and thought how appealing the High Guard executing the lecherous pig so the whole of the marches could watch. But there was a problem with this and that was the fact they had to get him to surrender either way. But the thought of him being beheaded by the High Guard was a nice and easy to swallow pill.

Then he spoke his mind, "Suicide the man is too much of a pig to kill himself".

Acentua agreed and agreed heartily. But if the money was on one way it would be suicide. And every one could feel the war being over (Well as close as it gets). Acentua gave the Reaper Leader a large sum of money, that being about seventy billion gold credits. The Reapers on the air hatch guarding the *Defiant* whistled as the credits were put on board. They then began to re-arm the *ESP* and the *Defiant* with nuclear space missiles. As well as sand for the thrower that was being used to hide their Ion trail.

Tiris finished the nights revelry and went and caught up on some much needed sleep. He then woke the next morning with a slight hang over. It didn't matter to Tiris as he asked the Reaper Teams one and two to check in. Making sure that they were fully sober and ready for the next leg in their journey of war. They had a tough fight as they knew exactly what was on the cards for them. They were going to hunt down Taxus and finish him and the Titan Reapers. Tiris knew a couple of ways to get at the Emperor Taxus and they were fiendish in their calculated plan of action.

One was called rogue quest, a secure way of getting close to the Emperor. It would need the *ESP* to limp spluttering next to Taxus and his emissary, who with all the luck and skill that came from Bucker, would limp as if it had just finished a battle with the trill. And come off worst. But this was just a decoy, once it gripped onto the Skiff, Bucker would open up the Air lock and hide in the *ESP*'s main venting. It would as this may turn out to be a ghost ship or so the Emperor and his council would take it to be. They would then notice it to be one of the Reapers vessels. At this they would proceed with caution. That's when the *Defiant* would come out of hiding and pulverise the Emperor and his squad of Titans.

This all went as planned, but somehow the Titans had the clairvoyance to see through this trick and threw in a thermal nuclear grenade. Bucker ejected out after leaving the ship and going out into zero gravity. Where he was spotted by the *Defiant* and a small life capsule was sent to him. He boarded the capsule and gripped for the *ESP* to explode with its nuclear weapons going up as the *ESP* was blown to bits. But the Emperor was clever and cleared away to a safe haven just out of the EMP range. He did this defiantly so, leaving it to the last minute to escape and evade the blast radius.

They didn't even notice Bucker as before he rendered himself to space he managed to put a dead man's pulse on the Skiff.

He then got back on board the *Defiant* and reported immediately to Tiris.

"You get the tracker positioned on the Imperial Skiff?" asked Tiris.

Bucker stood there breathing through his skull helmet, "Yes sir I got one before they destroyed the ship".

Bucker sighed and continued, "She was a nice ship, gonna miss her sir".

Tiris waved him to be dismissed. They then kept tabs on the Skiff. Following at a safe distance. They had every intention of destroying the Skiff and its occupants, but knew they had to make a move sooner rather than later. They shot off into deep space knowing that if the Skiff got to the human home-world of Terrar they would miss their chance. But Tiris was not holding back, he intended on destroying the Emperor and his Guard of Titans. So the *Defiant* sped off to head them off at the beginnings of the Terra system. This was going to get really ugly.

"First things first," said Tiris as he aimed a sidewinder space missile at the Thrusters at the rear of the ship. Then without hesitation he fired. And it crippled the ship. The *Defiant* then crept up beside the Skiff, and joined at an air lock. The reaper teams were both ready, this was it the final standoff between the raving madman of an Emperor and Tiris. They were caught out as they opened the air lock and a volley of laser repeaters were fired at the two squads of reapers, who barely noticed as there armour was fully powered,

And could take twice the amount of punishment than what was thrown at them. But this didn't make much difference as the Reaper squads were more mobile and that gave them a great advantage.

They could duck and dive the various weapons as they went off. Dayton as usual was controlling the spider mines that were taking away the legs of the Titans. But Dayton didn't have to many left as they were being used up quickly. But they were still the best plan of attack from the Reapers. After felling six or seven of the Titans they realised that they had luck on their side. But the Titans weren't going that easy. The Titans then used a volley of Plasma weapons that ripped into the first three of them rendering their armour useless. But still they fought. And also knew that these were Titans and held the aces in their hands. They were tougher and had more to lose in the grand scale of things. But this didn't stop Tiris's reapers from trying to kill the Titans. It would appear as if the Reapers were winning in the fight but that was just appearances.

No, the Titans held their ground and held it well with the destruction of the first three of the Reapers. That held them even and Tiris was looking for the ranking officer. Who was by all ends getting the skirmish to go his way. And Tiris knew this, so he had to locate the officer and destroy him anyway he could. He switched on his helmet AI and gave the command to find the markings of the officer. The AI had a little trouble, then suddenly Tiris was face to face with the Titan. And his helmet was targeting in a rush by the Titan. This scrambled the Colonel's targeting and Tiris was left with the only option, hand to hand. He wasn't scared, just knew it was going to be tough as they fired first their small arms, then they got down to knives. But the Titan had no idea what weakness's that the Reaper team had.

Tiris went straight for the Bio readout computer trying to send enough damage to cause the Titan to power down. But this was easier said than done. No, Tiris was running on blind luck as the Titan crushed the optics on the reaper. Tiris flipped his helmets kill switch then jettisoned his skull. He again tried to destroy the Titans main battery then remembered where the Trill had found a weakness. The base of the spine where the battery lay.

'Oh Cascoe you are not forgotten,' thought Tiris, then all of sudden he pulled out a magnetic grenade that would stick to the Titans power source. Then when he pushed the kill switch in his hand he would destroy the Titan. He told the rest of the reapers what to do and they all followed suit. Then they began to run away heading back to the *Defiant*. They got to the airlock and as the door shut Tiris let off a puff on his stogie, then flipped the cap and pushed the button, and they all laughed. As there was an almighty bang and crack as the skiff ruptured and the Titans were destroyed and left to float in the endless vacuum of space. They then circled the rest of the Skiff and fired three sidewinder space nuclear missiles at the rest of the Skiff that Taxus was on. Game over.

The End